"I Wouldn't Look At Me Like That If I Were You, Unless…"

Clark let the rest of his sentence trail off, but the message was clear.

"Sorry," Sara muttered, ducking her head.

This urban cowboy was toying with her affections big time, and she was wallowing in it like someone starving for love and attention. So why didn't she call a halt to this madness and insist he take her home? Now.

She licked her lips. "I'd…better go home."

He moved his head close to her face and whispered, "Not now."

"When?' she whispered back, swaying toward him.

He closed his arms around her. "After we make love."

Dear Reader,

Hey, look us over—our brand-new cover makes Silhouette Desire look more desirable than ever! And between the covers we're continuing to offer those powerful, passionate and provocative love stories featuring rugged heroes and spirited heroines.

Mary Lynn Baxter returns to Desire and locates our November MAN OF THE MONTH in the *Heart of Texas*, where a virgin heroine is wary of involvement with a younger man.

More heart-pounding excitement can be found in the next installment of the Desire miniseries TEXAS CATTLEMAN'S CLUB with *Secret Agent Dad* by Metsy Hingle. Undercover agent Blake Hunt loses his memory but gains adorable twin babies—and the heart of lovely widow Josie Walters!

Ever-popular Dixie Browning presents a romance in which opposites attract in *The Bride-in-Law*. Elizabeth Bevarly offers you *A Doctor in Her Stocking*, another entertaining story in her miniseries FROM HERE TO MATERNITY. *The Daddy Search* is Shawna Delacorte's story of a woman's search for the man she believes fathered her late sister's child. And a hero and heroine are in jeopardy on an island paradise in Kathleen Korbel's *Sail Away*.

Each and every month, Silhouette Desire offers you six exhilarating journeys into the seductive world of romance. So make a commitment to sensual love and treat yourself to all six!

Enjoy!

Joan Marlow Golan
Senior Editor, Silhouette Desire

Please address questions and book requests to:
Silhouette Reader Service
U.S.: 3010 Walden Ave., P.O. Box 1325, Buffalo, NY 14269
Canadian: P.O. Box 609, Fort Erie, Ont. L2A 5X3

Heart of Texas
MARY LYNN BAXTER

Silhouette Desire

Published by Silhouette Books
America's Publisher of Contemporary Romance

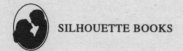 SILHOUETTE BOOKS

ISBN 0-373-76249-6

HEART OF TEXAS

Copyright © 1999 by Mary Lynn Baxter

Visit us at www.romance.net

Printed in U.S.A.

Books by Mary Lynn Baxter

Silhouette Desire

Shared Moments #24
Added Delight #527
Winter Heat #542
Slow Burn #571
Tall in the Saddle #660
Marriage, Diamond Style #679
And Baby Makes Perfect #727
Mike's Baby #781
Dancler's Woman #822
Saddle Up #991
Tight-Fittin' Jeans #1057
Slow Talkin' Texan #1177
Heart of Texas #1249

Silhouette Special Edition

All Our Tomorrows #9
Tears of Yesterday #31
Autumn Awakening #96
Between the Raindrops #360

Silhouette Intimate Moments

Another Kind of Love #19
Memories that Linger #52
Everything But Time #74
A Handful of Heaven #117
Price Above Rubies #130
When We Touch #156
Fool's Music #197
Moonbeams Aplenty #217
Knight Sparks #272
Wish Giver #296

Silhouette Books

Silhouette Christmas Stories 1992
"Joni's Magic"

36 Hours
Lightning Strikes

MARY LYNN BAXTER

A native Texan, Mary Lynn Baxter knew instinctively that books would occupy an important part of her life. Always an avid reader, she became a school librarian, then a bookstore owner, before writing her first novel.

Now Mary Lynn Baxter is an award-winning author who has written more than thirty novels, many of which have appeared on the *USA Today* bestseller list.

One

Sara Ann Wilson.

Her name had rattled around in Clark Garrison's mind since he'd left Houston and headed for River Oaks. Although he finally spoke the name aloud, he still couldn't believe the connection.

Why not? he asked himself as his Lexus sports utility vehicle hit the city limits of the small town—so small that it had only one caution light, a gas station and a grocery store of sorts. Some things, least of all small towns, never changed.

He didn't know anything about the ''grown-up'' Sara Wilson. All he remembered was that he had dated her younger sister, Alice, and that Alice's sister and mother hadn't particularly liked him.

Alice had never said as much, but he knew that Katherine Wilson had thought he wasn't good enough for Alice, that he was wild and unsupervised, the town's bad boy. A snarl curled Clark's lip. If she'd only known about her darling daughter—talk about wild.

As for Sara, he remembered very little, except that she'd been five years older than Alice and him, making her thirty-nine now. He racked his brain trying to recall what she looked like. No specifics came to mind other than she was tall and willowy and had auburn colored hair. She must not have been attractive or he would've remembered. A pretty face or a great body rarely got past him.

However, he did recall that Sara had been quiet and on the shy side, that she never seemed to have much to say. Smart. Alice always used to whine that Sara got all the brains in the family.

Not only did she have to be smart, but she had to have money to buy a nursing facility. Hell, as far as he knew she could be a millionaire, but he doubted that. In that postage-stamp-size town, there were no secrets.

It was open season on what went on behind closed doors. If Sara had come into a fortune, he would have heard it through the gossip pipeline. On second thought, maybe he wouldn't have, since neither one of them lived in River Oaks, hadn't for years.

After his boss, Lance Norton had given him the folder on the nursing facility, he'd had time only to glance at it, the owners' names popping up first thing: Don and Opal Merrick and Sara Wilson.

His plan had been to study the file in detail before leaving the office, but that plan had gone awry. He'd had several important calls on other pending deals that demanded his attention. Also he'd had correspondence to dictate to his secretary.

However, as soon as he reached his aunt's house, he would memorize everything in the file. His guns would definitely be loaded when he started on the hunt.

Business was booming, a fact that gave Clark the urge to pat himself on the back. He'd certainly done his share and more to make the company what it was today. But then, he was amply paid for what he did, not only in money but in stock. He had no kicks coming on that score.

One thing for sure, people would keep growing old, and the need for nursing homes and other special-care facilities would forever be in demand. And he planned to meet that demand, be Johnny-on-the-spot, to buy and sell those facilities in order to turn a profit.

Once he had himself a sizable nest egg, however, he'd always said he would retire. At thirty-four he had that goal already within reach. A grin teased Clark's mouth as he thought about his cattle ranch in East Texas where he planned to settle.

But he wasn't near ready to leave the city, to wake up to the sounds of nature instead of sounds of human beings. Maybe when he was too old to do anything except rock on the porch, he'd seriously consider making the move.

Yet there were times, like now, when he wished he were at the ranch helping his foreman Joe Hanover brand cattle, especially with the cool snap they were having, which accounted for his added energy.

However, that energy would be better used on the job he was sent here to do. Acquiring the nursing facility, Quiet Haven, and the surrounding land would be a real coup for Norton and Associates. He was the man who could pull that off.

In fact, this deal had the potential to be the biggest ever. An interstate was due eventually to go through the area which meant the property would be worth millions.

But it was imperative that he move fast while the news of the pending highway was still under wraps.

Now as he whipped his vehicle into his aunt's drive and killed the engine, he sat for a few minutes and stared at the place where he'd spent his teenage years after his parents' death in a house fire.

He knew Zelma had done the best she could with an orphaned boy who was headstrong and most times belligerent, who was more interested in kissing the girls than getting his lessons.

Not much had changed on that score, he thought with a cynical smile before reaching in the back seat for his briefcase. He stretched to grab the handle, as the case had shifted during the drive.

"Hellfire!"

That wrenching cry came from his toenails. His back! He'd thrown his back out again.

Clark cursed a blue streak, but it still didn't change the fact that he was frozen in pain, at least for the time being. But dammit, he had to move. He couldn't sit in the vehicle indefinitely.

Gritting his teeth and ignoring the sweat that poured profusely from his skin, he opened the door and eased his feet onto the ground. Bent to one side, he crept onto the porch and lowered himself gingerly onto the swing.

Nausea almost got the best of him before he could suck enough air into his lungs to stave it off. But the pain. Oh, the pain. He'd swear someone was poking him with a hot cattle prod.

He was in one helluva mess.

"Whoever you are, mister, you're on private property."

Clark smothered another curse, having recognized the stale voice right off. It belonged to Daisy Floyd, Zelma's neighbor, who was older than dirt, blinder than a bat and the biggest gossip in town. Oh, dear Lord, please deliver him. What had he done to deserve *her*?

He opened his eyes to find Daisy's wrinkled face peering at his, her cloudy blue eyes narrowed to slits and her false teeth not quite in place.

"Hello, Daisy," he managed to say, though it took almost all his existing energy.

"Is that you, sonny boy?" she yelled.

Clark cringed, having forgotten that she was deaf as a post to boot. "Yes, Daisy, it's me."

"What's the matter? You look plum green around the gills."

Maybe the old busybody wasn't as blind as he'd thought. Or maybe he looked worse than he thought. It didn't matter. Nothing mattered except finding some relief from the sharp, shooting pain.

"It's my back. I pulled it out of whack."

"How'd you do that?"

"How doesn't matter, Daisy," Clark said through clenched teeth and with as much patience as he could muster, which amounted to very little. He had to get rid of this pesky woman and do something, anything to get relief.

"Have you been to see Zelma up at the nursing home?"

"No, Daisy."

"Figures. You ain't never been concerned about her."

"I just got into town."

"That's no excuse. She asks for you all the time, you know?"

He didn't know, and now that he did, it made him feel worse. Guilt became another source of pain, but only for a second. Hell, he wasn't about to fall into that old gar hole and let Daisy Floyd jerk his chain as she'd done so many times in his youth.

He wouldn't be rude to this old lady, but he didn't intend to take any crap from her, either. He wasn't a teenager without a home any longer.

"Daisy, thanks for checking on me, but I know you have things to do."

"No, I don't," she said in a voice that sounded like scrunched up parchment.

Clark blew out a breath as another jolt of pain hit him. "Well, I do," he said, pushing his words through jaws that felt locked.

"What's wrong with your back, sonny?"

"I told you, I pulled it out. I have a bunch of messed up vertebraes."

"You need a doctor."

No joke, he wanted to lash out, but refrained. It wasn't her fault that he'd injured himself. Why didn't she go away and leave him alone to suffer in silence? But then, she'd never left them alone. His aunt hadn't liked her any more than he had.

"Since old Newt retired, I know there's not a doctor in this one-horse town."

"You watch your mouth, boy. There ain't nothin' wrong with this town, you hear?"

"You're right, Daisy. Now, if you'll excuse me—"

"We do have a doctor."

Clark's spirits brightened considerably, only to dim just as quickly. He couldn't believe the old bat knew what she was talking about. Surely another doctor in his right mind wouldn't set up practice here. But at this point, he'd settle for a good vet.

"Who and where is this doctor?" Clark asked in a tight voice.

Daisy beckoned with her head. "Down yonder."

"Where's down yonder?" His pain and his temper were fast reaching saturation level. He didn't know how much longer he could remain on an unsteady porch swing or put up with this aggravating old broad.

"On Windom Street. Six-nineteen to be exact."

"What's his name?"

"It ain't no he."

"You mean the doctor's a woman?"

"Yep. And she's a sight better than any doctor where you come from," Daisy continued, "if you're not too high and mighty to go to her, that is."

Clark let that one slide. Besides, this conversation had run its course. Even if he had to crawl back to his vehicle, he was getting rid of this woman.

"Her name's Dr. Wilson. Sara Wilson."

Daisy spoke with such pride in her voice that for a second the name didn't register. Then it hit him with the same vengeance as another burning prod to his back.

"Sara *Ann* Wilson?" he asked, dumbfounded.

"That's her," Daisy responded, pride deepening her voice.

Clark groaned inwardly. Was this really happening? Yes, and his misery wasn't near over yet. He was accustomed to the best sports doctors in the business working on his chronic back pain, which had been brought on by an old football injury from his college days. He didn't want this small-town doctor working on him, especially because he planned on having a business relationship with her.

Damn! Fate had definitely kicked him in the gut.

"She's one of them pull-and-stretch doctors."

"You mean chiropractor?"

"That's what I said."

Despite his condition, Clark almost laughed outright. Talk about a quirky twist of events, this was it. But not a good one, he told himself, trying to decide if he should crawl to his vehicle and attempt to make it back to Lufkin.

He moved slightly only to yelp out loud.

"You're in sad shape, sonny boy."

Clark glared at Daisy, then holding onto one arm of the swing, he staggered to his feet. However, that was as far as he could go.

"Want me to help you?" Daisy asked.

Hell, no! "Yes, if you wouldn't mind."

"Put your arm around my shoulders."

"I don't think that's a good idea."

Daisy pointed her finger in his face. "You always were one to argue with your elders. For once, just do as you're told."

"Yes, ma'am."

Somehow Daisy managed to help him inside the Lexus without further harm to him and without any to her. In fact, she was much stronger than she looked; he'd have to hand her that. She might be old, but she wasn't dead—far from it.

Minutes later he brought the vehicle to a stop in the doctor's driveway, then very gingerly made his way to the front door. But not without cost. A new onslaught of sweat drenched him, and he suspected his face was the color of paste.

He practically fell against the doorbell and stayed there. Yet it seemed an eternity before he heard any sound of life. If she wasn't at home, he didn't know what he'd do.

The door swung open.

"Yes?" a soft voice asked before her eyes widened and her mouth fell open.

"Sorry to disturb you," Clark said in a low, terse voice, "but I'm—"

"In pain. That's obvious."

Clark clamped his jaw shut, another pain spasming his back.

"Clark Garrison, right?"

Before he could respond to the fact that she recognized him after all these years, a wave of dizziness swept over him, and he pitched forward into her arms.

Her gasp was the last thing he remembered.

Two

Later Sara couldn't have said how she remained upright, much less got this six-foot-two lug of a man to the floor without causing further injuries. An added miracle was that she positioned him on his back.

If she hadn't seen his twisted features, she would have sworn he was drunk, something that wouldn't have surprised her, considering who he was and what she knew about him.

Although it had been years since she'd seen him, she would have recognized him anywhere. His appearance hadn't changed all that much except that he had gotten better looking, if that was possible. Alice and every other girl her age had thought he was the greatest thing since sliced bread. These days Sara suspected that *women* thought the same thing.

Now, however, was not the time to rehash what a conceited "bad boy" her sister's ex-boyfriend had been. Her job was to revive him and relieve his pain as quickly as she could.

At this point Sara couldn't say who was perspiring the most, him or her. Geez, she'd had some memorable moments in her tenure as a chiropractor, but this one would go down in the history books as the most bizarre to date.

A smile unwittingly tugged at her lips. Wasn't it supposed to be every woman's secret dream to have a gorgeous man fall at her feet? While she had no such dream, she could appreciate the moment.

"Clark, Clark," she said, "can you hear me?"

He grunted, then nodded.

Relief surged through her. "Welcome back."

"Yeah, right."

Apparently he hadn't lost total consciousness which was good and bad. His tolerance for pain, it seemed, was quite low, a weakness found in many of her male patients. "Can you tell me, or better yet, pinpoint where you hurt the most?"

There were a million other questions she would've liked to ask, such as how had he known who she was and where she lived. But those questions were easily answered. In a town the size of River Oaks, nothing was sacred.

He seemed comfortable, sprawled on the carpet that covered her hardwood floor. At least he was no longer moaning, and a semblance of color had returned to his face.

"The cattle prod's right here." Clark rolled onto his stomach, grimacing, and placed his hand in the middle of his lower back.

His analogy brought another smile to Sara's lips, although she knew exactly what he was saying. In order to understand back pain, one had to have experienced it. She certainly had. That was one of the reasons she had chosen this profession.

"Let's see if we can't get rid of that prod," she said, "but I'm making no promises. This situation is far from ideal, but then, I don't have to tell you that."

"Dammit, lady, just do what you gotta do, okay?"

"I have a table in my spare bedroom. You think you could make it in there?"

"Do I have to?"

Sara picked up on his shallow breathing at the same time she noticed the muscles in his jaw were bunched. "No. I think I can make an adjustment right here and work the kink out. A hard surface is what we need, and the floor certainly is that."

"Go for it." He cursed. "Otherwise, I'm not sure I'm going to live through this."

Sara hid a smile. "Oh, I suspect you'll live. I'm good at what I do."

"Let us pray."

"Your shirt has to come off," Sara said calmly but crisply, ignoring his ill humor and crankiness.

He struggled onto his elbows. Between the two of

them, the shirt was soon off and tossed aside. Once he was again flat on his stomach with head to one side, she knelt and placed her hands on his upper back, then began a slow, deliberate descent down toward his lower back, touching, pressing in what she knew were just the right spots.

He moaned.

"Am I hurting you?"

"God, no," he rasped. "Please don't stop. Your hands feel like magic."

Sara had had her hands on numerous bodies, most of them male due to the numerous ranching and farming jobs around River Oaks. Never once had she experienced any stimulation whatsoever. Until now. Suddenly, she was light-headed, and her mouth was dry as her hands massaged his muscles.

Maybe it was because she knew him from back when, knew that he had been in her house, knew that he had dated Alice, knew that he had possibly been *intimate* with her sister.

The latter thought rocked her to the core. So what if he'd fooled around with her sister? It was nothing to her. It hadn't been then and it sure wasn't now.

Clark moaned again as her hands touched the right spot directly above his waistline. Sara watched as the hard, tanned muscles rippled and quivered underneath her fingers. What a great body, she thought, feeling her mind jump back on that runaway train headed down that forbidden track.

The first time Clark Garrison walked into their old rambling house on Vine Street, which had long since been sold, her breath had almost stopped. She would never forget that moment. His confident swagger and devilish smile had brightened their dreary kitchen like a dose of unfiltered sunlight.

She had remembered thinking, If only he was older and she was prettier, maybe he would've stared at her with those hungry eyes instead of her sister.

Stop it! Sara chided herself, feeling her face flame and hearing him yelp. "Sorry," she muttered. "I didn't mean to hurt you."

"You hit the place." His words came out a grunt, and she noticed new patches of sweat on the exposed side of his face.

"I want you to roll over. Your knee needs to come up to your waist," Sara told him, her tone all business now. "The pain will be severe at first, then it'll taper off."

"I know," he ground out. "That's what my doctor does at home."

Once she had the knee where she wanted it, cupped into his waist, and her hands back on his flesh, she felt the knotted muscles give way.

"Ahhh," he moaned.

"Better?"

Clark blew out a long breath. "You bet."

"Think you can sit up?"

"I know I can."

Sara stood. "Once you're upright, we'll head for the sofa. I want to put some heat on that area."

It wasn't near the ordeal Sara suspected it would be, though again he was a big man. Still, he was agile and not at all cumbersome on his feet. That was what had made him an all-state athlete in school.

Within seconds after he was up, Clark was sitting on the couch with his head back and his eyes closed.

"Are you all right?" Sara asked, scrutinizing him closely.

His eyes popped open, and he squinted up at her. "You should know."

"In that case, you're welcome."

"Patting yourself on the back, huh?"

"Self congratulations aren't quite in order," she finally said. "You still have to get up and walk out of here before I can do that."

That mocking smile she also remembered softened his heretofore tense lips. Talk about sex appeal—he seemed to ooze it, a scar under his right eye, another trophy from his football days, heightening that appeal.

She couldn't say that he was handsome. He wasn't. His features were too irregular, yet somehow they worked, especially in conjunction with his unkempt sandy-colored hair, great physique, tanned skin and brilliant blue eyes. They were all undeniable pluses. With those, a man's face didn't have to be perfect.

Suddenly Sara felt self-conscious, thinking how awful she must look, only to jerk herself back in hand. It didn't matter how *she* looked. He was a onetime patient—nothing more, nothing less. "Hold still while I get the heating pad."

"You don't have to worry about that. I'm afraid to move."

"Don't be." Sara's lips twitched. "We can do it all over again, you know."

"I'll pass," he said tightly.

She turned and walked toward her makeshift office. When she reached the room, her heart was beating far faster than it should have been. *Damn!*

Not bad, not bad at all, Clark thought as he watched Sara make her way out of the room, at least not from the back. If nothing else, her derriere was intriguing, moving in perfect rhythm with her every step. Yet she was uptight, except when she'd had her hands on him, he corrected himself.

He jerked his gaze off her and let a few expletives fly. What the hell was wrong with him? He knew, though he hated to admit it. There was touching and there was *touching*.

His insides vibrated just thinking about the sensations that had run rampant through his body everywhere she touched. He hadn't been lying, no siree, when he'd said she had magic fingers.

He wondered what they would feel like on another part of his body. He swore, his face tightening as if he had lockjaw. Thinking of her in terms of sex was the last thing he needed. It was bad enough that he'd had to come to her for treatment, in light of why he was in town.

On the other hand, he couldn't look a gift horse in the mouth. Because of who she was, she had saved him from having either to return to Houston or go to the hospital in Lufkin. Once she put the heat to his back, he was convinced he'd be as good as new. Oh, he'd be sore for a few days, unable to brand any cattle, but he could live without that.

Besides, he hadn't come to town to play with his cows. He'd come to land a coup that would make him rich. He wasn't about to let anything mess that up, certainly not his libido.

Yet when Sara walked back into the room, he couldn't seem to take his eyes off her. What galled him was the fact that she wasn't even conventionally pretty.

She wasn't homely, either.

Because her face was devoid of makeup, he could see her great bone structure—high cheekbones and wide-set green eyes. Her skin was incredible, too— a milky white that appeared as smooth as a baby's butt.

Her hair was an odd color, somewhere between auburn and light chocolate, which added to her allure. She wore it in a short, straight style that accented her long neck.

But it was her body that was the attention grabber. Although extremely slender and tall, she had more than ample breasts, breasts that even her loose-fitting caftan couldn't hide. He wished he could see her waist; he'd bet his hands would fit around it.

Still, she wasn't the type of woman he had ever been attracted to. So why the sudden fixation with her? he asked himself, but got no answer.

Feeling desperate to elevate his thoughts to the impersonal level, Clark blurted out the first thing that came to mind. "How much do I owe you?"

She stiffened visibly. "Nothing at the moment. I suggest you come for another treatment, but in my office."

His eyebrows shot up. "You really think that's necessary?"

"Absolutely." She paused, giving him a cool, pointed look. "Unless you want your back to go out again."

"You know better than that," he muttered crossly. But he dreaded another session because her magic hands messed with his mind.

"Wise man."

"Whatever the doctor says."

Her professional facade didn't slip one iota. "Since that's settled, let's get this heating pad behind you so it can get to work."

She plugged it in near where he was sitting, then placed it behind his back. Although she had been close to him earlier, he'd been in too much pain to notice how fresh and sweet she smelled. Now her scent hit him in the face like a slap. He sucked in his breath and held it.

She stepped back and peered down at him. "Are you in pain again?"

"Uh, no," he said, turning away, unable to meet her eyes, especially with his manhood rallying around his thoughts.

"Would you care for coffee or something else to drink?" Her tone was polite but emotionless.

"Uh, no, thanks."

Sara sat in the chair adjacent to him, and for a moment an uneasy silence fell between them. It was one of the few times he had ever been at a loss for words. But then, he'd never been in quite such a precarious situation.

He tried to concentrate on her homey but tastefully decorated home while the heat seeped into his back, but he couldn't. He was too conscious of *her*.

"Do you mind me asking what brings you back to River Oaks?"

"My ranch," he said off the top of his head, then kicked himself mentally. Why the hell didn't he tell her the truth?

She gave him a disapproving look, which raised his ire and his curiosity.

"I was hoping you'd come to see about your aunt."

That flat statement tightened his gut, as well as the noose around his neck. "That, too, of course."

"She's a sweetheart, you know? I see her almost every day when I visit my mother, who's also in the nursing home."

"I appreciate that a lot." Tell her, dammit. But the words still wouldn't come. They stuck in his throat.

"She would appreciate seeing *you* a lot more."

While her criticism was wrapped in soft words, he felt the sting nonetheless, a feeling he didn't like.

"Look, I've intruded enough on your time. It's late, and I know you have to work tomorrow."

"That I do."

Blessedly, he got to his feet without mishap. "Thanks again for everything. I feel like a heel for—"

Sara held up her hand, stopping his flow of words. "Forget it. You're not the first to appear on my doorstep at an ungodly hour, nor will you be the last."

"At least you're a good sport about it."

She shrugged. "I consider that part of my job."

He stared at her a long moment, trying to figure out what was really going on behind those lovely green eyes. Though she met his gaze, he learned nothing. The woman was one cool cookie who either had his number or didn't didn't give a damn. Maybe she disliked men in general, or just him in specific.

If the latter was the case, then he was in deep trouble. Somehow he had to figure out a way to do some damage control. But before he could say anything else, she had reached the door and had it open.

"Good night, Clark Garrison. It was nice seeing you again."

He didn't believe that for a second. "Same here, Dr. Wilson," he said, walking out the door.

Once outside he cursed a blue streak.

Three

***

"**Y**ou old son of a gun, how've you been?"

Clark slapped his foreman, Joe Hanover, on the arm while pumping his hand.

Joe gave him a wide grin that exposed the gaping hole in front where two permanent teeth should've been. The remaining teeth were nicotine coated, as Joe smoked like a chimney on the coldest of winter days.

Even so, his health was good, so good that to Clark's knowledge he'd never missed a day's work. But with Joe, looks could be deceiving.

Though short and wiry, his foreman was as tough as the cowhide he took care of on a daily basis. In addition, he could do most anything with his hands from plumbing to carpentry work.

Clark shuddered to think of what he would do without his foreman. If nothing else, Joe was invaluable because Clark was rarely able to get to the ranch. He depended sorely on Joe to keep things up and running.

"I'm tolerable," Joe finally responded, following several deep drags on a cigarette before dropping, then crushing it with a scuff-toed boot. "I sure as hell wasn't expecting you anytime soon."

"I wasn't expecting to be here, either. I stayed at Zelma's place in town last night and thought I'd stop in this morning for a look around the ranch."

Joe shoved the brim of his soiled hat back. "So, what's up?"

"Business, actually."

"Well, whatever, I'm shore glad to see you, 'cept you don't look so good."

"I had a bad night. The old back nailed me."

"Man, that's too bad."

Clark's mouth curved down. "Yeah, it is. And it's something I'm going to have to learn to live with."

Joe merely shook his head.

Clark turned away, his eyes roaming over his treasured domain, taking in pastureland as far as the eye could see, all dotted with cattle. Then he turned and noticed the ranch house sitting atop a hill.

The white paint that covered it sparkled in the morning sunlight. The last time he'd taken a vacation, he and Joe had made some much needed repairs to the rambling old house, making it livable, if not cozy.

"You stayin' for a while?" Joe asked.

"I'm not sure. Right now, though, I have to go, but I'll be back later."

Joe waved his hand. "I'll be here. I'm starting to brand that new herd we got last week."

"Again, I sure appreciate you taking care of that for me," Clark said, hearing the longing in his own voice.

A friend from Lufkin had called and said he was selling off his herd and had wanted to know if he was interested. Clark had said yes without hesitation. But he'd been unable to get away; too much was going on. Of course he'd called Joe, who had said, No sweat, boss.

Apparently, it hadn't been any sweat, as the new cattle were chomping on his grass with the same vengeance as hogs on slop. Clark felt envious of Joe and his relatively uncomplicated life.

Hell, he'd like to be dressed in his grubs the same as Joe and work with him, tagging the cattle with the Garrison Ranch brand.

One of these days, Clark told himself.

"Look, you don't have to thank me," Joe said. "I'm just doing the job I love."

Clark smiled, then slapped him on the shoulder again. "Just don't ever quit on me."

"I'd be a crazy man to do that." Joe grinned. "Hell, you pay too much."

Clark laughed. "I'll see you later."

Once Clark was back in his utility vehicle, he took one more look around the place, sighed, then drove off. When he'd awakened earlier that morning, he'd been afraid to move for fear his back would freeze up on him again.

It hadn't, thanks to the doc with the magic fingers. Thoughts of Sara and the evening before had jumped to the front of his mind in vivid detail, and he'd groaned. He couldn't afford emotionally or monetarily to think about Sara Wilson in any capacity other than that of a doctor and a businesswoman. Yet the fact that she was part owner of the facility he was sent there to purchase had definitely rattled his cage.

Earlier that morning, instead of dwelling on the predicament he was in, he'd gotten out of bed, showered and, over several cups of coffee, had read the entire file concerning the facility and the owners. The information had been sketchy, but he wasn't worried. All he needed to know was how to get the owners' names on the dotted line of a sales contract.

With that uppermost in his mind, Clark had intended to head straight for the nursing facility, eager to scope it out. And with his aunt Zelma residing there, he had every right to be on hand and do all the snooping he wanted without raising any suspicion.

However, at the last minute, he'd decided to run by the ranch, eager to see that, as well. Now as he drove through the arched gates of Quiet Haven, to say he was impressed with what he saw would be an understatement.

This was indeed a prototype facility, one Norton and Associates just had to have. Excitement coursed through Clark as he parked the vehicle and got out. The outside, surrounded by gardens, both flower and vegetable, was awesome. When he walked inside, he pulled up short, equally impressed.

He hadn't a clue whether it was Sara or the Merricks or both who were responsible for the building and the decor. No matter, it was damn well done. So far he hadn't seen a nursing home that could equal this one, and he'd only stepped inside the front door.

To the right and left of the entryway were two spacious living areas with nice furniture and game tables. In both of the rooms, residents were milling about. Clark knew from the blueprint of the facility that it was comprised of three wings. First off, he needed to locate the unit where his aunt resided.

Suddenly he felt a tug on his arm, followed by a small voice saying, "Mister."

Clark swung around to find a tiny lady with watery eyes staring up him. He smiled. "Yes, ma'am?"

"Do you know where I live?"

"No, ma'am, I don't," Clark said uneasily, not used to dealing with the residents themselves.

Her lower lip quivered.

"But I bet I can find out and take you home," Clark said quickly, sensing she was about to burst into tears.

Her uneven features brightened. "Oh, thank you."

Before he'd taken two steps, a nurse approached them. "Sir, are you a relative of Mrs. Mary's?"

"No, I'm not," Clark answered in a soft tone.

"I didn't think so." The nurse gave him a lame

smile, then placed her arm around the lady's shoulders. "Come on, Mary, I'll take you to your room."

Clark swallowed a hard sigh as he strode forward to the nurses' station, where he asked directions to Zelma's room. Once there, he found his aunt sitting in a chair sound asleep. He pulled another chair beside his aunt's, but didn't wake her, trying to come to grips with the change in her. She seemed to have shriveled up, nothing like the tall, strapping woman she used to be, who could and would take a belt to him whenever she thought necessary.

Considering he had turned into a responsible citizen, after all, he guessed she had done the right thing, though at the time he'd resented her.

"Aunt Zelma," he whispered, shaking her gently on the arm.

Her eyes fluttered open, and she stared at him through glazed, empty eyes.

"It's me, Sonny."

"Sonny," she repeated, then smiled.

"Yeah, Sonny, your nephew. Don't you remember?"

She smiled again. "Do you like my dress?"

Clark's heart lurched as he looked at what she was wearing. That was when he noticed she had on not one, but two dresses. He shook his head, thinking he couldn't handle much more of this. "Uh, your dress is lovely."

"Now, who are you?" Zelma asked before her head lobbed back and her eyes closed.

He patted her awkwardly on the arm, then watched helplessly while her chest moved up and down.

"Mrs. Gillispie, you're going to be just fine."

The woman's round face stretched into a grin. "Oh, thank you, thank you, Doctor. I don't know what I would've done without you."

Sara smiled. "I'm just glad it was muscle spasms in your back and nothing more serious."

"You can forget Dr. Sara taking any praise, Mrs. Gillispie. She's not about to. There's something in her makeup that forbids such a thing."

Sara gave her nurse Rosa Foster one of her "looks," but Rosa, as usual, paid her no heed.

"Don't you agree?" Rosa asked the woman.

"I sure do, honey," Mrs. Gillispie responded, her gaze steadfast on Sara. "But it doesn't matter, we'll sing her praises, anyway."

"I just did my job like I do every day of the week, like any other chiropractor worth her salt does."

Mrs. Gillispie had stepped into the cubicle to dress, but that didn't stop her from commenting. "Well, I for one don't know what River Oaks would do without you, especially the way these cattlemen and farmers around here are always pulling something out of whack."

"Well, again, Mrs. Gillispie," Sara said mildly, "I appreciate your loyalty. If you have any more problems, give me a call."

"You can count on that, Doctor."

Once the woman had left the office, Rosa said,

"Oh, by the way, Mrs. Gillispie was our last patient."

Sara peered at her watch and noticed it was only four-thirty. She'd have time to visit her mother and get home before dark, which would be a rarity.

With it being early October, the days were shorter, so when she got a chance to leave early, she took it. Today was no exception.

"Thanks for the unexpected break," she told Rosa.

"Do you ever regret coming back here?" Rosa's eyes narrowed on her. "In Dallas you had a great place to live and a lucrative practice, not to mention all those single guys running loose."

Sara didn't hesitate. "No, absolutely not."

"You're indeed one in a million, my friend, because there's nothing here for a lovely, single woman like you."

"I'm not lovely, and I enjoy being single."

"You are lovely and you have a dynamite body, which—"

"Enough, Rosa!"

Rosa's pretty features sobered. "I hope I didn't offend you. I know you have your mother and the home—"

"Hey, no offense taken. Forget it. I'll see you tomorrow. Give your kiddos a hug for me."

"Will do."

Once in her office, Sara shut the door and took a deep breath. While she adored Rosa, who was invaluable in her dual role as nurse and office manager, she could be a handful at times. Yet Sara often envied that wild streak in Rosa, knowing she was far too much the other way—too quiet and too much a loner.

When she had left Dallas and returned to the small community outside of Lufkin, she had run into Rosa at the post office. They had caught up on old times, and before she'd gotten her stamps, Rosa had been hired.

Sara hadn't regretted that impulsive decision, a rarity for her, and that had been three years ago. Her practice had grown steadily. Much of that growth was due to Rosa who told everyone about the clinic.

Still, it hadn't grown enough. Sara wasn't sure it ever would, at least not enough to enable her to pay off her huge bank note on the nursing facility in which she was part owner.

When she'd been knocking down that big salary in Dallas, meeting the note hadn't been a problem. But now her situation was different.

Sara frowned, trying to steer her thoughts in another direction. She didn't want to think about that burden. It was much too depressing and frightening to dwell on how she was going to juggle her finances each month to meet her obligations.

Rubbing the back of her neck, Sara removed her white coat and hung it up. Then grabbing her purse, she dashed out the back door.

Four

Sara stopped and perused her surroundings. Due to certain state guidelines, Quiet Haven had been designed for function, not beauty. But the grounds were a different matter altogether. The landscaping, including flower gardens filled with seasonal annuals of all colors, sizes and shapes, was breathtaking.

Sara found herself actually holding her breath as her eyes focused on a huge bed of pansies. Their bright, multicolored faces seemed to be staring right at her.

Realizing she was wasting time, Sara shifted her Camry in gear once again and drove around to the back, parked and walked inside where she was once again filled with pride. To think this upscale facility, consisting of three wings all under one roof—skilled nursing which included Alzheimer's patients, regular residents and assisted-living efficiency apartments—was part hers.

Though Quiet Haven was already five years old, it had the appearance of just having opened. That was due to the way it was run, something Sara and her partners were in total agreement about. Cleanliness and quality care was their motto.

The personal and financial sacrifices she had made in order to become an owner were well worth it, more so now, since this was where her mother would likely live out the rest of her life.

With thoughts of Katherine in mind, Sara increased her pace and headed toward her mother's large corner room in the assisted-living wing. As she passed down the carpeted hall, she saw several women with canes and walkers. She smiled and spoke a few words to each before moving on.

Finally reaching her mother's door, Sara opened it. Katherine was sitting in her favorite rocker, facing the garden.

"Mamma."

Katherine Wilson swiveled, and when she saw her daughter a smile brightened her face. "Hi, darling. Come in."

Sara crossed to her mother's side, leaned over and kissed a rouged cheek, then eased into an adjacent chair. "So, how was your day? Any pain in the old hip?"

"Not too bad."

Sara sighed. "You wouldn't tell me if the pain was excruciating."

"Now, now, you know better than that," Katherine admonished in a soft, gentle tone.

Sara grabbed a fragile blue-veined hand and held it. If she had any regrets, it was where her mother was concerned. The reason she had left Dallas in the first place was to take care of Katherine after she fell and broke a hip.

However, when her mother was released from the rehab unit at the hospital, she refused to live with Sara or let anyone live with her. Much to Sara's chagrin, it was Katherine's choice to move into Quiet Haven. Even her younger sister Alice, who lived in St. Louis with her family, hadn't been able to persuade her mother to change her mind.

So far Katherine seemed to have no regrets. And while Sara would've preferred to have had things her way, she had learned to respect, if not accept, her mother's desire for independence.

"How are you today, my dear?" Katherine asked in her soft voice.

"Busy."

"That's wonderful."

Sara squeezed her mother's hand, thinking what an attractive woman she still was, even though she was in her late sixties. Like her, Katherine was tall but with a much stouter frame that was now slightly bent from osteoporosis. Still, her hair was thick and a lush color of gray that matched her eyes.

While she might look weak and fragile, she

wasn't. She was headstrong to a fault, a fact Sara had difficulty with as Katherine was her underpinnings; her daddy having died of a heart attack years earlier. Because Alice lived so far away, it sometimes seemed as if she didn't have a sister, that it was just her and her mother.

"Why don't you have supper with me?" Katherine's eyes held a teasing glint. "We're having lasagna."

Sara wrinkled her nose. "My least favorite, which you well know."

"Well, you can't blame me for trying. It certainly wouldn't hurt you to put some meat on those thin bones."

"Don't you start. Rosa's already been on my case today."

"About what?"

"Oh, the usual," Sara hedged, wishing she'd kept her mouth shut. While her mother's body was failing, her mind was as sharp as ever.

"She worries about you being alone just like I do."

"Now, Mother, don't start. I'm fine the way I am."

"That's absurd. You don't have a life. All you do is tend to the sick and afflicted both at the office and here."

Sara laughed.

"It's not funny, especially when the only man in your life is older than your mother and a codger to boot."

"Why, Mother, I can't believe you're talking about Uncle Newt like that, especially someone who's been and still is a lifelong friend."

Newton Frazier was a retired chiropractor who had become her mentor and whom she visited on a regular basis.

"That's the problem. He's my friend and shouldn't be yours. Besides, he's not a good influence on you."

Sara laughed and shook her head. "That makes absolutely no sense. If it weren't for Uncle Newt, I wouldn't have this practice and you know it."

"You're right, of course, but you need to be around young people, not us old folks all the time."

"You let me worry about that, okay? Besides, I'm trying to convince Newt to move here. He's getting too old and much too feeble to live alone."

Her mother gave an unladylike snort. "Good luck. His head's as hard as yours."

Sara hid her smile. "Look, I'm happy with my life the way it is. So give me a break. Now, about my sister, have you heard from her lately?"

"As a matter of fact, I got a letter today."

"How are things with them?"

Katherine suddenly looked troubled. "I can't quite put my finger on it, but I sense all is not well between her and Dennis."

"That's nothing new. You know Alice—if there isn't a crisis in the making, she's not happy."

"That's not a nice thing to say."

Sara shrugged. "It's the truth. Anyhow, if there is trouble, they'll straighten it out. They always do."

"You're right. It's just that I was hoping she and the kids could pay us a visit."

"Maybe they can," Sara said, dropping her mother's hand and rising to her feet. "I have to run, Mamma."

"But, honey, you just got here."

Sara leaned over and grazed Katherine's cheek with her lips. "I know, but I have some errands to run."

"Of course you do, darling. Don't pay any attention to this selfish old woman."

"You may be old, but you're not selfish," Sara returned in a teasing voice.

"Are you all right?"

Sara was taken aback by the sudden and unexpected question. "Why do you ask?"

Katherine's forehead wrinkled into a frown. "I don't know, really. You just look tired, as if you didn't sleep."

Sara hadn't, but she didn't intend to tell her mother that. Her encounter with Clark Garrison had preyed on her mind until the wee hours of the morning. She wondered how he'd fared this morning, if his back remained in place. If not, she was sure she'd know soon enough.

"I'm okay, Mamma. You worry too much."

"You need a man friend."

"Oops, now I know it's time to go."

"Sorry," Katherine said.

"No, you're not, but I guess that's why I love you."

Katherine gestured with her hand. "Go on, skedaddle, get out of here."

Sara was still shaking her head when she passed by Zelma's room only to stop dead in her tracks and blink. As if he sensed he was being watched, Clark looked toward the door. When he saw her, he stood and walked toward her.

"You look surprised," he said without preamble.

"I am."

His mouth tensed. "I told you I came to see my aunt."

"So you did."

"She doesn't seem to be doing all that well."

"She hasn't for a long time now."

He flushed, which meant her barb had hit its mark.

"Look, I know how you feel about me, but—"

"I don't think you do," Sara said flatly.

"You know what I meant."

Though he tried to temper his tone, Sara picked up on his suppressed impatience and anger. It was clear he was out of his element here, and she wasn't helping any. But he *had* neglected his aunt, and to her way of thinking, there was no excuse for that. She hadn't mollycoddled him last night, and she wasn't about to start now.

"Aren't you going to ask about my back?"

Sara gave a start at the sudden change in his voice. It seemed lower and somewhat more conciliatory, if not on the intimate side.

Her face suffused with color. "The fact that you're up and about answers that."

He didn't respond, which only seemed to thicken the tension between them, as their eyes met and held for a moment.

Sara was the first to speak. "I have to go."

"This is a great place you've got here."

"I know," she said with confidence.

He chuckled, which did something funny to her insides. "Look, I'll see you later," she said.

"I'm counting on it."

Sara was still thinking about that last statement when she entered the administrator's office, feeling as though she didn't quite have the upper hand, a feeling she despised.

"Hi, Doc."

"How are things?" Sara asked.

"Just dandy."

Sara stared at Edwin Turner as she sat down in the chair in front of his desk. He was in his early thirties with dark hair and dark eyes and lots of nervous energy that he put to good use. He'd been administrator since the home opened, and Sara couldn't have been more pleased with his performance. He bonded with the elderly as did she; that was what it took to make such a place run on greased wheels.

"If things are dandy, then the food must be good this week," she said with a forced smile.

Edwin grinned. "You got it. The cook's in fine form these days."

"Thank heavens for that."

As a rule, the food was one of the biggest factors the home had to deal with. And while Edwin didn't bother her or the Merricks with the day-to-day problems, Sara made it her business to keep on top of things. It was easy, because she came to see her mother every day. The Merricks weren't that involved or interested, which was fine with her.

"You on your way back home?" Edwin asked into the silence.

"Shortly. I forgot to give Mother the new knitting needles I bought for her. I'm headed back to her room, then to the house." Sara paused, her features sobering. "I've been thinking."

Edwin's face sobered. "About what?"

"The need to put our heads together and come up with a plan to get this place filled to capacity."

Although Clark's unexpected presence had certainly dominated her thoughts, she hadn't forgotten her depressing financial situation. While filling all the empty rooms in the facility wouldn't totally solve that problem, it would help.

Edwin sighed. "I couldn't agree more. It's high time we reached that goal. What beats me is why we haven't. By now we should have a waiting list a mile long."

"I wouldn't go so far as to say that, but again, we do need to talk. I'll be in touch."

Sara had just reached her mother's room when she heard the laughter. For the second time that evening she stopped in her tracks.

Clark? In her mother's room?

If she hadn't seen the two of them together with her own eyes, she would not have believed it. To make matters worse, they were laughing and chatting like they were long-lost friends, something that couldn't have been further from the truth, or at least that was the way it was at one time.

Disconcerted, Sara stood in the doorway. Both turned and looked at her.

Katherine was the first to speak. "Why, darling, I thought you were gone."

"I forgot your needles," Sara said in a strained voice, her gaze on Clark, who seemed to shift uncomfortably in his chair. Or was that her imagination?

"Clark just happened to stumble on my room and was kind enough to stop by and visit."

It was all Sara could do not to keep from blurting out that at one time her mother would have thrown him out if he'd showed his face around her or Alice.

"Your mother hasn't changed at all," Clark said. "She's still as feisty as ever."

Katherine laughed. Sara wanted to throw up.

As if he sensed Sara's acute displeasure, Clark stood, though he made no effort to leave or show any repentance. In fact, that mocking smile hovered about his lips, setting Sara's teeth on edge even more.

"Go on, honey. Clark won't bite me."

Sara didn't see the humor in this at all and didn't know why. God, she was acting like a prune-faced old maid, and she hated herself for that.

"I guess I'll see you tomorrow, then," Clark said, "at the clinic."

"Make an appointment," she demanded churlishly, then turned on her heels and walked out.

Five

"**W**hat do you want to do, Sara?"

Sara chewed on her lower lip while cradling the phone in the crook of her shoulder. "I don't see that I have a choice, do you?"

Her banker and friend, Duke Kissler, let out a sigh. "Not unless you just happen to win the lottery or something."

His attempt at humor fell on deaf ears. This had not been a good day, and it wasn't going to get any better. But she couldn't take her mounting frustrations out on this man. He was her ally, having been instrumental in pushing her loan through on the care facility, a gesture that was now causing her problems, but one she didn't regret.

Still, to be called and told your business account was overdrawn was humilitating to say the least. How had she let that happen?

"Sara?"

"I'm here."

"So, I'm to transfer more of your personal savings into that account, right?"

"Right."

He was quiet for a moment. "What are you going to do when your savings are depleted?"

A sharp pang hit Sara. "I don't have a clue." Although she realized that wasn't an adequate or responsible answer, it was the best she could do under the circumstances.

"Well, you know I'll do what I can to help."

"I know you will, Duke, but you've already gone above and beyond the call of duty."

"Something will come up. You wait and see."

"I hope so, because I don't intend to give up my share of the facility."

"That kind of attitude's half the battle, young lady."

"Thanks, Duke. And thanks again for taking care of me. I'll be in touch."

Once she was off the phone, Sara ran her hands through her hair, then patted the mussed strands back in place. Even though her financial situation was grim and getting grimmer, she still had enough money in savings to make her banknote on Quiet Haven for several more months. Thus, she wasn't going to dwell on the future. Besides, this day and this next appointment must have her undivided attention.

Clark Garrison.

A groan almost escaped her. Glancing at her watch, she noticed it was time for him now, which meant he was probably in the waiting room. Something told her he would be prompt.

"Yo."

Sara looked up. Rosa was standing in the door, her face animated and her eyes twinkling. After shutting the door, she crossed to the desk.

"Don't say it, Rosa."

Rosa seemed taken aback for a moment only to recover with a broadening smile. "You think so, too, huh?"

"Think what?" Sara asked in an innocent tone, but she knew exactly what was whirling through Rosa's mind.

"That he's a hunk—Richard Gere style, no less."

"You're married," Sara responded inanely.

"I may be married, but, hell, I'm not dead."

"Cute."

"Who is this guy, anyway?"

Sara let go of a pent-up breath. "It's a long story."

"I'll settle for the short version," Rosa said impishly, "at least for now."

"He's a businessman from Houston here to see his aunt."

"And?"

Sara didn't bother to curb her growing impatience. "And he used to date my sister, Alice."

"Ah, so you really do know him?"

"Yes."

Rosa gnawed at the lipstick on her lower lip and cocked her head to one side. "Why do I think you're hiding something?"

"Because you're paranoid."

"Oh, really?"

"Look, we're wasting time, and you know how I feel about keeping patients waiting. Here's Mr. Garrison's chart."

Rosa gave Sara an incredulous look. "See, I knew you were hiding something."

"Rosa, it's all in the file. Read it, but first get an X ray of his back. I want to see that at the same time I see him."

Still grinning, Rosa paused at the door and swung around. "Is he married?"

"I haven't the foggiest," Sara declared stiffly. "And what's more, I don't give a rip."

"If he's available, he wouldn't be too young for you, you know."

"Out!"

Undaunted, Rosa's grin spread. "Hold your drawer tails, I'm going."

The second the door closed behind her assistant, Sara lunged out of her chair, wishing she were anywhere but here. What was wrong with being unmarried? Not one damn thing, she told herself.

So why did everyone think she was something out of a sideshow because she wasn't married with 3.2

children? Small-town mentality. But that wasn't her excuse; she knew better.

So why was *she* feeling so badly about herself? That question she couldn't answer, nor was she going to try. She wouldn't give it another thought. She was content with herself and her life. She didn't need a man to make her complete, despite what everyone else thought.

The tap on the door jerked her back to the moment at hand. Rosa walked in with the X rays and gave them to her. "He's ready when you are."

"Send him in." Sara then clipped the pictures on the backlit board and perused them.

"How does it look, Doc?"

That low gravelly voice sent an unexpected chill down her spine, which made her stiffen. After taking a deep breath, she turned around only to widen her eyes. Instead of putting the short gown on where it tied in the back, Clark had done just the opposite. The garment was open down the front, exposing the hairs on his chest all the way down to his tapered waistline.

To add insult to injury, his lips were split in an off-center grin, adding to his raw attractiveness, something Sara would just as soon not be aware of.

"Like your nerves and muscles have been in a meat grinder, actually," she forced herself to say in her most professional manner.

"That pretty much slam-dunks it."

"How does your back feel now?"

"Not great, but it's been worse. The other night for starters."

Sara strode up to him, getting a whiff of his cologne along with another dose of *that* smile. She couldn't put her finger on what there was about this man that both intrigued her and set her teeth on edge. Perhaps it was his cocky attitude, his overbearing self-assurance. Or perhaps her fascination stemmed from past and present gossip.

The reputation he'd had when he dated Alice had continued to dog him in the form of gossip, though she hadn't paid much attention to it. Now that he had stepped back into her life, she recalled bits and pieces of the beauty-shop smut—his marriage and divorce, his high style of living and his stable of women.

"What's on the agenda for today?"

By the time she stopped her woolgathering, Clark had gotten on the table and was watching her closely. For a moment she couldn't help but wonder what was going through his mind.

Then shaking herself mentally, she said, "I'm going to work around and down your entire back, concentrating on that bad spot, of course."

Once he was on his stomach, Sara pushed the gown up around his shoulders. The instant she placed her hands on his rock-hard muscles, she felt a quiver dart through him.

"God, that hurts so good," he muttered.

Sara didn't say anything. She couldn't. To her shock and mortification, it was taking all her wits and concentration not to turn this adjustment therapy into a massage session.

Geez, what was happening to her? She wanted to yank her hands off his flesh as if it was poisonous yet she wanted to caress it at the same time.

"Is this painful?" she forced out, putting pressure on a spot at the base of his spine.

"Yes," he said in a deep voice, almost a growl.

She peered down at him and saw that his face had drained of color. "Your backbone is still out of alignment, though the swelling has lessened."

"I don't want any pain pills. They make me climb the walls."

"I wasn't going to offer you any."

"So what's the verdict?"

"As soon as you get back to Houston, visit your doctor. He'll tell you what your options are."

"I know what he'll say. I want your opinion."

"That's not necessary," Sara said in what she hoped was a professional but off-putting tone. She wasn't his doctor and didn't want to be. The sooner she could get rid of him, the better.

Finally she removed her hands, but not before spending time on the muscles at the base of his neck which she knew would relieve the pressure on the entire back area.

"Let's see if you can get into a sitting position by yourself," she said, stepping back.

In a gingerly fashion, he rolled onto his side that faced her, then sat upright. "A piece of cake."

She suspected that wasn't entirely the case, but

then, who was she to argue? Actually, she'd like nothing better than to think she would never have to see him again, much less touch him, even though that's what she did for a living. But no matter how much she needed the money and the patients, she'd pass on future business with Clark Garrison.

"Your talents are wasted in this small town."

Sara blinked, noticing that he was now standing close to her. Too close. She stepped back, a gesture he apparently didn't miss, for his eyes narrowed.

"I don't think that's any concern of yours," she said in a slightly shaky voice.

"Probably not," he said easily, his gaze trapping hers.

Though Sara met his direct look, it wasn't easy. She wanted to turn away, especially when those eyes seemed to smolder, as if he was mentally undressing her.

Feeling her face flood with color, she turned away, hoping he hadn't noticed her reaction. Damn him!

By the time she reached her desk, picked up his chart and scribbled some notes, he was buttoning his shirt. Her insides relaxed, knowing this ordeal was over and that she wouldn't have to see him again. Avoiding him at the nursing home would be easy.

"Say, are you busy tonight?"

Her head came up. "Excuse me?"

"I said are you busy tonight?"

"That depends," she said, sounding as though she had run out of breath.

"I'd like to take you to dinner."

Stunned was too mild a word to define the reaction that stampeded through Sara. In fact, she was so stunned that she couldn't speak. She simply stood transfixed and continued to stare at him.

He grinned. "Don't look so shocked."

"I don't—"

Clark angled his head, his grin widening. "It's a perfectly innocent invitation."

Sara's open mouth snapped shut, and just as she was collecting herself to respond, he added in his high-handed manner, "I'll pick you up at eight sharp."

With that, he walked out the door.

Six

"**I**t's about time you showed up."

Sara leaned over and kissed her old friend Newton Frazier on his prickly face. "Mmm, quit shaving, huh?"

Newton glared at her, then shifted around in his recliner. "Now, don't go gettin' on your soapbox. I only shave every other day. And you know why, too."

"The razor tears up your face." Sara smiled as she sat down on the sofa across from him. "If you'd get an electric one, you wouldn't have that problem."

"Ah, hell, I don't need none of those fancy gadgets."

"Okay, you old hardheaded coot, I'll keep my mouth shut."

Newton chuckled, and when he did, Sara noticed another tooth was missing. He wouldn't get fitted for a dental bridge, either. But then at eighty, she guessed he could do just about anything he wanted and get by with it.

Despite his obvious physical flaws and his age, he still cut a striking figure. He was tall and thin, but not too thin. And though his hair was not as thick as it used to be, it was a beautiful white. That, combined with his blue eyes, never failed to turn heads.

He had never married, though he'd been in love several times, he'd told her. However, none of those affairs had ended in a march down the aisle. As she grew older, Sara could understand why. It would have taken a special kind of woman to have lived with Newton.

Her family friend and mentor definitely marched to his own drummer, which for the most part was out of step with everyone else. One either accepted him as he was or not at all. She not only accepted him, she loved him dearly—warts and all.

But she worried about him. His heart had been acting up along with his arthritis. She wouldn't be surprised to walk in and find him on the floor. That thought sent a chill through her.

If it hadn't been for Newton, she wouldn't have been a chiropractor. When he was in practice, she used to visit his office with her daddy, who always seemed to have something out of joint. Uncle Newt would let her watch him work the kinks out, something that had fascinated her and still did.

"So what's been going on with you, girlie?"

"Oh, this and that," Sara said, not sure exactly how much of the truth she wanted to share. Yet wasn't that why she'd come? As close as she was to her mother, there were some things she couldn't talk to her about, especially her mixed feelings concerning Clark. Even though her mother had been chatting with him on a friendly level, she doubted Katherine would be that excited if she knew—

Knew what? Sara asked herself, irritated at the turn her mind had taken.

"I'm waitin'."

Newt's crusty voice brought her back to the moment at hand.

"Actually, I just came to see you," Sara said, lying through her teeth.

"Poppycock," he declared. "I know that look on your face and in your eyes."

"Darn it, Uncle Newt, you don't know everything."

"Might, near it," he countered in his matter-of-fact tone.

Sara smiled, then shook her head. "You're impossible."

"That's part of my charm."

Sara rolled her eyes. "That it is."

"Before we get into a serious discussion, why don't you get us some coffee. I just made a fresh pot."

Sara peered at her watch. "I guess I have time for at least one cup."

Newton frowned. "What's your all-fired hurry?"

"Work, for one thing."

A few minutes later they were drinking from their cups in silence, though she felt Newton scrutinizing her closely.

Finally he broke the silence. "Something's gnawing at you, and I want to know what it is."

Sara leaned over and placed her cup on the coffee table between them. When she straightened, she averted her gaze out the window where she saw a hummingbird feeder hanging on a low tree branch.

"Stop stalling, girlie."

Sara returned her attention to Newton, though she hated continually to burden him with her problems. But he wouldn't have it any other way, she knew. Besides, he didn't have anyone else to worry about or care for. And everyone needed someone.

"For starters, I'm in a bit of a financial bind." That hadn't been what she intended to say. For the life of her, she couldn't say what made her blurt it out.

"That doesn't have to be a problem. I can loan—"

"No." Sara's tone was emphatic.

"Like hell, you say. I can do anything I want."

Sara laughed without humor. "Not this time. This is my mess, and I'll clean it up."

"How?"

"My savings aren't depleted yet."

"It's the note on the home, right?"

"Right."

"If my memory serves me correctly, you told me you could handle that."

"I could at the time. But then I was in Dallas knocking down a huge salary with a huge savings account." She paused. "Of course, it took a chunk of that as a downpayment on the facility."

"Neither the facility nor your practice is pulling its own weight."

"That's it in a nutshell."

"You have the option to sell, you know. The nursing home, that is."

Sara's eyes flashed. "Never!"

"All right, girlie, just simmer down. I know how you feel about the home and tending to the elderly. Hell, I'm living proof of that side of you."

"Somehow things will work out. It just makes me feel better to talk about it."

"Well, again, you know I don't have much in savings, having never made much, but you're welcome to what little I do have."

"I'm not taking your money and that's that."

He shrugged and was silent for a moment, then said, "What else is bothering you? Is it a patient?"

Again Sara laughed a humorless laugh. "I think you missed your calling, Uncle Newt. You should've been a psychiatrist."

"Poppycock," he said again. "Ain't got no use for shrinks. So, is it a patient?"

"Yes and no."

"That's clear as mud. Yes and no, what and who?"

Sara smiled, feeling his offbeat humor work its magic. She felt herself relax for the first time since she'd awakened that morning and realized she was supposed to see Clark again that evening.

"Do you remember Clark Garrison? He dated Alice years ago."

"That name sorta rings a bell. Why?"

"Well, he's back in town."

"As a patient?"

Sara sighed, beginning to feel the panic building inside her again. "Of sorts. An old football injury flared up, and I worked on him."

"Did he get out of line?" Newton demanded in a fierce tone. "Because if he did—"

"He didn't. He asked me to dinner, but I'm not going." There, she'd said it, all without so much as taking a breath.

Newton threw his head back and laughed. When he looked at her again, his eyes were twinkling. "Of course you're going."

"No way."

"And just why not?"

"For one thing, he's younger than me—five years to be exact."

"So what? That's the 'in' thing these days."

"Just how would you know that?"

"Hell, I may be a recluse, but even I watch those talk shows on TV."

Sara attempted to smile. "No matter. He's just

passing through, checking on his aunt at the home, to be exact.''

"Which should be right up your alley—here today and gone tomorrow.''

"All the more reason not to fool with him.''

"Ah, hell, go on and have a good time,'' Newt said, flapping a hand. "It'll do you good to go out to dinner, have a man's company for a change, instead of us old fogies.''

"You sound like Mother. Taking care of old fogies, as you call yourself, is what I love to do and what I do best.''

"Baloney. You need men friends. In fact, it's not too late for you to get married. I know that's what Katherine wants and I do, too.''

"You can forget that. I'm not interested.''

And she wasn't. She had given up on ever having a man of her own much less marrying and having children. Her career seemed to have taken precedence over everything else. Now at thirty-nine, she was convinced her biological clock was no longer ticking. That fact saddened her, but since she was practically minded, she had accepted she would never have a family of her own.

"*Hardheaded* isn't the word for you. I'd just as soon talk to a box of rocks. I'd get a more intelligent response.''

Sara chuckled, then stood. "Settle down, you old coot, before your blood pressure rises. I'm a grown woman who has to do what she has to do.''

"That doesn't make it right.''

"It's not right that you won't move to Quiet Haven so you won't be alone and where you'll be cared for properly."

Newt snorted. "Don't start on that again. I'm going from this house to the cemetery."

"You're impossible."

"Truthful, is the way I see it."

Sara kissed him again on the cheek. And when he would've gotten up, she placed a hand on his bony shoulder. "Stay put. I can see my way out."

"Don't stay away so long," he muttered, scowling up at her.

"You're just spoiled, that's all," she teased, then walked outside where her laughter instantly faded into a frown. Facing her was the task of tracking down Clark and telling him she wasn't going to dinner with him.

But he had the rejection coming, she thought in defense of her decision, having stridden out of her office as though all he had to do was say jump and she'd ask how high.

In your dreams, bud.

Clark sat in the living room of his aunt's house, feeling almost like his old self, thanks to Sara Wilson.

Ah, Sara. He sipped from his glass of tea, recalling the shocked look on her face when he'd issued that dinner invitation out of the blue. Not only had she appeared shocked, but bumfuzzled as well.

Interesting.

He'd be willing to bet she didn't see anyone. Who was there to see here seriously? Oh, he surmised there might be a Farmer Brown who would be interested in having her share his bed. But that wasn't going to happen; he'd figured that out right off the bat. While Sara might live in the country, *she* wasn't country.

In fact, she was one classy lady, one he would very much have liked to get to know had the circumstances been different. That touch-me-not attitude of hers was the kind of challenge he liked in a woman, a challenge a lot of men liked.

So why hadn't she ever married? Apparently her attitude was a turnoff to the men around these parts. That was because she had never touched them.

Even now Clark couldn't block out of his mind how her fingers had felt on his flesh, how he'd ached for them to keep going lower. And lower.

Give it a rest, Garrison, he warned. She was off-limits on all levels other than business, and he damn well knew it. It was bad enough that his back had gone south and he'd had to turn to her for help.

But what was done was done, and he couldn't undo it. What he could do was soften her up a bit with a nice dinner, a bottle of great wine and entertaining conversation before revealing why he was really there and what he wanted. Then he'd move in for the kill, so to speak.

If the truth were known, Sara was probably head over heels in debt, though there was nothing personal in the file to indicate that about her or the Merricks.

Still, he knew what an upscale facility of that size cost—a big chunk of change.

Most people who bought nursing homes were monied people or corporations. Somehow, he didn't think that was the case with Sara. The Merricks, on the other hand, probably fit that scenario.

Thinking about the Merricks made him reach for the phone and dial their number. Once he told Sara he was there to purchase Quiet Haven, he would be ready to meet with the Merricks.

He waited while the phone rang several times, only then to hear a voice mail message saying the Merricks were out of the country and would be for another week.

"Damn!"

The only up side to this latest twist was that it would give him longer to butter up Sara Wilson, something he wasn't comfortable with, but had to do.

After having visited Quiet Haven and learning what a jewel it truly was in terms of its location and the property surrounding it, he couldn't return to Houston without a signed deal.

With that thought in mind, Clark punched out another number, the company's investigator, Phil Cohen.

"Hey, it's Clark," he said in response to the gravelly voice on the other end. "Got a job for you."

"Shoot."

"Find out everything you can about a Dr. Sara Ann Wilson, especially her financial situation."

"Consider it done."

"But be discreet, okay? This is a touchy subject. I'm in a touchy spot."

Phil chuckled. "What else is new?"

"Go to hell."

"You're welcome."

Once the receiver was back in place, Clark smiled, then turned his attention to the file folder on his lap.

Seven

The country club restaurant in Lufkin was both lovely and quiet. Sara looked around, taking in the room with its tastefully decorated tables and plush, high-backed chairs. Her gaze then wandered to the long span of windows where she concentrated on the softly lit and perfected grounds.

Come morning, she knew those grounds would be littered with golfers and golf carts.

She and Clark had given the waiter their drink orders and were waiting to receive them.

"Have you ever been here before?"

Clark's question forced her to face him, something she had purposely avoided since he'd arrived on her doorstep sharply at eight o'clock. "No, actually, I haven't."

A thick eyebrow quirked. "That surprises me."

"Why?"

He shrugged with a lopsided smile. "I just figured you and some friends would've had lunch here."

"I don't do lunch out, nor do I have that many friends." God, but did she sound like a prickly bore or what? Why couldn't she loosen up?

"Doesn't sound like you have much fun, Sara Wilson." That lopsided smile didn't budge. "I wonder why that is."

She suspected he was attempting to make inane conversation to lighten her mood, but Sara couldn't relax. Instead, she sat like a cardboard figure, those blue eyes holding her captive, though she had no idea what lurked behind them.

"I'm either working at the clinic or at the nursing facility," she said stiffly.

"That's too bad."

"I happen to think it's good."

The other eyebrow quirked before he leaned forward and said in a low tone, "Relax. I'm harmless, you know."

Yeah, like an irritated shark. If possible, Sara's face turned redder but she rallied to the cause and smiled.

"Well, I'll be damned, you actually smiled and your face didn't break."

Sara threw him a look, though a semblance of that smile remained. "It's been a long day," she said by way of a lame explanation.

"I was beginning to think it was me," he quipped.

Sheer force of will kept Sara from flinching. It *was* him. She hadn't intended to come. When she arrived home from Newt's, she'd had every intention of tracking Clark down and telling him the dinner was off.

She never made that call. Even now she still didn't know why. She rarely let anyone railroad her into doing something she didn't want to do. But for a reason she couldn't explain, this man had managed to find a vulnerable spot and hone in on it.

She wanted to be with him, yet she didn't. Figure that. To worsen the situation, she'd actually worried about what to wear, as if it made a difference. In the end, though, she hadn't had a choice. She'd had only one suitable outfit in her closet and that was a simple black dress with a scooped neck and a slit up the side.

"Ah, now we can get serious."

Clark's voice responding to the waiter who had brought their drinks forced her out of her reverie. Once their wineglasses were filled and the bottle back in the ice bucket, they gave him their dinner selection.

After he left, they sipped on their wine while the silence grew. Finally Clark asked, "Is the wine okay?"

"It's wonderful."

"Good."

He took another healthy sip and when he did, Sara's gaze locked on his hand that circled the glass. It was a large but slender hand with a sprinkling of hair on the back. Suddenly she wondered how many women's bodies it had touched.

Mortified at that unbidden thought, Sara took a large sip of her wine, only to promptly choke.

"Are you all right?" Clark demanded, his eyebrows knit in a frown.

Sara coughed into her napkin, then dabbed at her eyes. "It went down the wrong way."

"That happens," he said easily.

Sara turned away again, trying to pull herself back together. If she continued to be that uptight, she wouldn't last another five minutes, much less the entire evening.

"By the way, did I tell you how nice you look?"

Sara felt his eyes linger on her breasts and for a moment, she was immobilized. Then she forced a smile. "No, but thanks."

A flicker of impatience darkened his eyes, and she knew it was justified. "You think I'm full of it, don't you?"

She gave him an incredulous look while scrambling to make a comeback. "Excuse me?"

"You heard what I said and know exactly what I mean."

"Actually, I don't know anything about you," she said in a stilted tone, feeling much more secure now that the topic of conversation was no longer how she looked. Even this hostility was an improvement.

"And from the vibes I'm getting, you don't want to, either."

Sara sighed and set her glass down. "You want me to be honest?"

His eyes narrowed. "I wouldn't have it any other way."

"Then what's your motive?"

"Motive? For what?"

"For asking me out."

He looked genuinely surprised. "Since when does a guy have to have a motive for asking a woman to dinner?"

Sara ignored his question and asked another of her own. "Is it boredom?"

Clark made a strangling sound, but before he could say anything, she went on, "Or are you out to give the town's old maid a thrill?"

His smile mocked her. "First of all, you're not old."

"I'm older than you—five years to be exact."

"Big deal."

"It would be to some men."

"Well, I'm me, and I don't give a damn."

"Wrinkles are imminent," she pressed in a small voice.

"So, I've already got them," he declared with a threatening grin.

She sighed. "You have an answer for everything, don't you?"

"Hell, you worry too much. Why can't you just go with the flow?"

"Ah, the flow." Sara touched her lips with the tip of her tongue. "Just kick back with the man who used to date my little sister, is that what you're saying?''

''Yeah, that's exactly what I'm saying.''

''I wish it were that simple.''

He snorted. ''It is that simple, only you want to make it complicated, which is crazy.''

''Maybe so, but...'' She let her voice trail off, knowing that he would get the message. Chances were good that he'd up and take her home. If so, she wouldn't blame him.

''No buts,'' he said, ''just get over it.''

Unwittingly a genuine laugh erupted through Sara's taut lips. ''You're a mighty persuasive and self-confident man, Mr. Garrison.''

''And you're mighty stubborn and lovely, Dr. Wilson, when you laugh, that is.''

Sara's heart raced, and she swallowed as his eyes held hers. ''Are you by any chance flirting with me now?''

''And if I am?''

She averted her gaze, feeling her heart race even more. ''You'll be wasting your time.''

''You let me worry about that.''

His thickly spoken words dragged her gaze back to him. He was staring at her now with those hungry eyes, which brought a deep flush to her face.

As if sensing he'd gone too far, he said in a smooth but guarded tone, ''So how *is* your sister these days? I bet she's married with children.''

''You're right,'' Sara said in a slightly breathy tone. ''They're in St. Louis.''

"Which means you and Katherine don't see much of them."

"Mother grieves over that, but that's the way it is."

Sara was uncomfortable discussing Alice with him. Maybe it was the idea of him touching her sister with those hands, kissing her...

"So how's your back?" she asked, her tone still out of kilter to her dismay.

"Holding together, thanks to you."

The waiter chose that moment to deliver their meal. Sara had ordered grilled fish which subsequently melted in her mouth, though she was surprised she hadn't choked on the first bite. But then she was hungry, not having had much to eat that day. Clark was eating his steak with the same enthusiasm.

They ate in silence, which more than suited Sara, as she was still having a hard time going with the flow of the evening. Clark Garrison set her nerves on edge. He made her aware of herself as a woman, especially when he looked at her in his certain way, as if he could see every dent and curve underneath her dress, especially her breasts.

No wonder her mother hadn't wanted Alice to date him.

"What are you thinking about?" Clark asked, shoving his plate aside.

"Oh, this and that," she said vaguely, feeling her cheeks grow hot again.

He chuckled. "You're definitely a hard one to figure, Doc."

"Don't waste your time trying," she shot back lightly.

"And if I want to?"

Oh, brother. "You'll be wasting your time," she said in what she hoped was a convincing tone.

Clark merely shook his head, but there was a twinkle in his eye when the waiter stepped up and removed their plates. After they passed on desserts but opted for coffee, the young man filled their cups along with their wineglasses, then disappeared.

"So tell me about the nursing facility."

Clark had put his cup down and was sort of slouched in his chair, looking casual but sexy as hell in an open-necked, cream-colored sports shirt and tan jacket, staring at her again as if she were the only woman in the world.

She wasn't used to men looking at her like that. What she couldn't figure out was his motive. She knew she wasn't his type, never had been and never would be.

Feeling back on solid ground, she asked, "What specifically do you want to know?"

He gave a casual shrug. "For starters, what made you want to own a nursing home?"

"I don't really know, except that I've always been interested in the elderly. When I worked in Dallas, I helped with several organizations that catered to them."

"Was it you who initiated the building of Quiet Haven?"

Sara laughed, and when she did, his eyes narrowed

and he grinned back, which robbed her of her next breath. God, those eyes and smile were a lethal combination. Finally recovering, she went on, "Heavens, no. It was the Merricks, Opal and Don, who mentioned the need for a nursing facility in this county, then added they were interested in building one. From then on, the idea snowballed and the results are the rest of that story."

"What does Merrick do for a living?"

"Nothing now. He made his money in the oil business."

"I see."

"I'm glad you're taking an interest in Quiet Haven, especially since Zelma's there."

"I know you don't approve of the way I've handled that situation."

"I didn't say that."

He grinned. "Yes, you did. Again. But that's okay. No doubt I deserve a slap on the wrist."

"As long as I'm alive and able, Zelma will be looked after."

"I appreciate that, but I intend to assume my responsibility."

"Oh, really?"

"Yeah. When I retire, I'm moving to the ranch."

Sara felt her mouth drop open. "You can't be serious."

"Oh, I'm serious, all right."

"You act as if that's going to be soon. You're far too young to retire."

"Right, but time flies."

"I find it hard to believe you'd ever be happy living here."

"Like you said earlier, you don't know me." His eyes were delving again.

Sara's skin prickled. "You're right, I don't."

However, she did sense that he'd be just as much at home in a pair of jeans, frayed shirt and boots as he was in silk suit, tie and Gucci shoes.

"So what do you plan to retire from? What kind of job, I mean?"

"I work for a large corporation," he said, "with its fingers in a lot of pies."

"Which means you'll be leaving River Oak soon." She made a flat statement of fact.

"I haven't decided that yet."

It wasn't so much what he said as the way he said it that spoke volumes. While he didn't mind grilling her, he didn't want to reciprocate. Fine. She didn't care anyway. He wouldn't be around much longer.

Even if he never left, it wouldn't matter. This man was too complicated and mysterious for her to become involved with. If she ever married, it would be to someone much less flashy and overtly confident than Clark, someone who shared her simple tastes and values.

"Are you ready?"

She shook herself. "Yes."

Silence prevailed the entire way back to her house. When he braked the car, she turned to thank him. But the words jammed in her throat as he was staring at her with those smoldering, but guarded, eyes.

"Look, I want to see you again," he said.

She shook her head vigorously while fighting down a surge of panic. "I don't think that's a good idea at all."

"Why not?"

She gulped. "Because."

"Because why?" he pressed, leaning forward.

"If your back needs attention, then, of course, I'll see you. Otherwise—"

"To hell with my back," he muttered thickly.

Wild-eyed, she latched on to the door handle, "I have to—"

"No, you don't," he ground out, then pulled her against him, pressing warm, moist lips against hers.

Eight

Sara was so stunned she remained unyielding in his arms. However, her ears were drumming and her heart was pounding, especially when his tongue skillfully nudged her lips apart. She was lost. And to her dismay she found herself responding.

She had no idea how long the hot, savage kiss lasted. It didn't matter. What mattered was that she had turned into a willing accomplice under his expertise.

It was when she heard a pitiful moan coming from somewhere deep inside her that the kiss ended as abruptly as it had begun. To add to her dismay, Clark was the one who pulled away, and with such force that he yelped, then grabbed his side.

"Dammit!" The word seemed to have come from the depth of his toes.

"Clark, are you all right?"

"No," he grunted. "Hell, no."

The streetlamp positioned above the vehicle allowed her to see his face. It was scrunched in pain. His back. Oh, Lord, he had popped his back out again.

If she hadn't wanted to brain him for causing a meltdown inside her from that kiss, she would have laughed, thinking it served him right for taking advantage of her.

Instead of lambasting him, though, she spoke very quietly and calmly. "Can you move?"

"I don't have any choice, do I?" His voice shook.

"There's always a choice," Sara said more to herself than to him, that kiss still clouding her mind.

"Will you help me out?"

Before Sara moved to open the door on her side, she took another look at him. Sweat was mixed in with the pronounced lines on his face. His lips, those same lips that had launched an assault on her senses a moment ago, were in a pencil-thin line.

"Don't do anything until I tell you," she said, scrambling out and dashing around to his side of the vehicle.

"Damn!" he said again, his harsh voice sounding like a shot in the quiet evening air.

"Don't talk, either," she ordered. "Save your energy. You're going to need it getting into the house."

"Can't you get the kink out here? I doubt I can make it inside."

"Yes, you can. If not, I'll have to call an ambulance."

"Over my dead body," he spat, then groaned again.

"If that's what it takes."

He cursed again, which Sara ignored.

Even though she knew his back felt like someone was using it as a dartboard, he still wanted to be in control. She had news for him. He was in no shape to make any decisions. She was the one calling the shots.

Somehow, much like the other time his back went out, she managed to keep hold of him. Now, however, the table was her destination. But again, he sagged heavily against her just inside the front door.

"Let me go," he pleaded, his voice pinched in agony.

Sara tightened her hold on him. "No floor tonight."

"I'm too heavy for you."

"You let me worry about that."

Sara's mind moved quickly. He was indeed heavy, and she didn't know how much longer she could remain strong and upright. If they both fell... No. She wouldn't entertain that thought for another second. She would simply do what she had to do.

Sara quickly assessed her options. Try for the table as planned or settle for the couch? It didn't take her long to make up her mind.

"We're headed for the sofa," she said, her breath and her arms giving way.

Grim-faced, he nodded.

Shortly, and much to her relief, he was finally down, his coat off, his shirt up and one side of his face buried in a cushion.

Ignoring her own palpitating heart and damp body, Sara touched his back, putting as much pressure on it as she dared.

He jumped, then groaned.

"Bear with me."

She watched her hands move over his quivering flesh, pressing, kneading, massaging.

"God, that hurts so good."

"You said that before."

He didn't respond. Instead he shut his eyes and took several deep breaths.

"Hold still. I'm going to get you a couple of natural muscle relaxers made from herbs."

He lifted his head slightly, only to grimace. "I don't want any pills."

"Yes, you do," she countered calmly. "Trust me on that."

When she rose to her feet, he positioned himself on his elbows.

"Ah, so it is better," she said.

"I think I might even live."

"I've heard that before, too." She paused and looked at him for a long moment. "Stay put, you hear?"

When she made her way back into the den a few

seconds later, Clark was sitting upright. Wordlessly she handed him the pills and the glass of water.

"I'd rather not," he said in a quarrelsome tone.

"I know, but I'm the doctor."

He gave her a dark frown, but he took them nonetheless.

"Now might not be the time to say this," she told him, sitting on the edge of the nearest chair, "but you should seriously consider having surgery."

Clark grimaced but not from pain, she knew, but rather out of frustration. "That's not going to happen."

"That remains to be seen."

Following her words, an uncomfortable silence ensued. Sara's thoughts jumped back to the kiss and she suspected his had, too. What a mess.

"Look, it's late," he said brusquely. "And I know you have to work tomorrow."

He tried to stand, and when he did, Sara darted across to him. "Whoa, take it easy."

"It doesn't look like I have much of a choice," he muttered tersely.

"How do you feel?"

"Woozy, dammit, like I've been on a ten-day drunk."

"It's those pills. They're taking effect."

Clark shook his head as if to clear it. "I hope I make it back to Aunt Zelma's."

"That's not a good idea."

His eyes narrowed. "So what are you suggesting?"

The air turned as hard and thick as a block of wood.

"That you stay here," she said, not looking at him.

"You'd let me?"

No doubt he was taken aback by her offer. Truthfully, she was too. In fact she couldn't believe she'd suggested it. But as a doctor, she realized it was the only safe and medically sound thing to do.

That didn't mean she liked it, though.

"You take the bed. I'll sleep here on the sofa."

"I don't think so."

Sara stood and peered down at him with flashing eyes. "It's unnegotiable."

"Like hell it is."

She ignored his comeback. "My bed is hard as a brickbat which is what you need."

"That's not going to—"

"Happen," she finished the sentence for him. "Oh, yes, it is.

Clark reached down for his shirt, only to sway. She reached his side in time to steady him. "This way." Her tone brooked no argument.

"Dammit, I don't like this." His tone was gritty and hard.

Sara refused to look at him, especially as he still had his shirt off, his broad chest and tanned muscles upfront and center in her face, not to mention that his belt was undone, as well. With her pulse beating ninety to nothing, she yanked the spread back on the bed.

"I hope you're able to sleep," she said.

"Dammit—"

"Please, just lie down. I'm the doctor, remember."

"Yeah, yeah."

His surly attitude finally got the best of her, and her eyes flashed again. "Look, I don't like this any better than you, but under the circumstances we both have to make the best of a bad situation."

Since it was obvious he knew exactly what circumstances she was referring to, his face darkened even more, but he didn't argue. Instead, he sat on the side of the bed, then very gingerly lay back.

Once he was flat, she pulled the sheet and light blanket over him, still careful not to meet his eyes, though she felt sure he could see and hear her heart hammering in her chest.

"How's that?" she asked, stepping back.

"Fine." He paused, then said, "Thanks."

Their eyes met and held for an awkward moment. Then she said, "If you need me, just holler."

"I won't," he muttered.

"I'll leave the door cracked, anyway." With that, she turned and walked out of the room on less than steady legs.

Sleep.

That luxury was something that eluded her. Sara had stared at the ceiling and counted sheep until she was tempted to say *baa-baa* out loud.

That idiotic thought almost made her giggle. She

clamped her hand over her mouth, fearing she would awaken Clark who was, of course, the reason she couldn't sleep.

Dammit, she resented him and what he was doing to her mentally and physically. How dare he waltz into her well-greased personal life and throw a cog in the wheel? How dare he *kiss* her?

The only problem she wanted to deal with was how to hold on to her share of Quiet Haven. She certainly didn't want to contend with a man who made her feel all quivery inside when she touched him, which ironically was her job.

Unshed tears filled her eyes. It wasn't fair. But then life wasn't fair or at thirty-nine she'd be married with a family of her own.

Suddenly Sara felt a keen dislike for the man who occupied her bed, convinced that he was merely using her to relieve his boredom.

"Well, to heck with him and the horse he rode in on," Sara mumbled, flopping over on her side which wasn't any more comfortable than lying on her back.

What to do?

She didn't know the answer to that. One thing she did know, he needed to get the hell out of Dodge, go back where he belonged. Another thing she knew, he wasn't going to kiss her again.

Even though the predawn light was dim and she wasn't in front of a mirror, she knew her face was pale as if she had a virus. And her stomach—that was exactly how it felt, too. But she wouldn't give in to her emotions. She wouldn't let him yank her chain to such an extent that she lost control.

Soon he would be gone and out of her life. Clinging to that promise, she closed her eyes.

"Sara."

That voice. She recognized it. But where was it coming from? Her next breath froze in her throat. She knew. Clark Garrison had stayed overnight in her house. *In her bed.*

Her eyes flew open. He was standing in the doorway to the living room, leaning against the jamb. Quickly she sat up, dragging the blanket with her, and pushed her hair out of her eyes. Humiliated beyond imagination, she knew she must look like someone out of a horror magazine.

"Good morning," he said.

She licked her cotton-dry lips. "How…did you make the night?"

"Like a baby. How 'bout you?"

"All right," she said in a weak tone.

"I doubt that," he said, moving deeper into the room, his gaze seeming to roam her body, a body that, thank goodness, remained fully clothed.

Still, she felt herself flush under his scrutiny and was barely able to answer in a coherent manner. "So how's your back?"

"I'm upright."

Sara scrambled to her feet and forced herself to look him in the eye. "From now on, if you have any more trouble, I think you should see a medical doctor."

"Oh? Why is that?"

"I can't help you anymore."

"Can't or won't?"

She lifted her head definitely. "I've made my decision."

"What if I don't want to see a medical doctor?"

"Clark—"

"It's because I kissed you, isn't it?"

Her face drained of color but she held her ground. "That has nothing to do with my decision."

"You're lying," he said in a low, gravelly tone. "But no matter, I don't want to change doctors." He paused. "I happen to like the way your hands feel on my flesh."

Sara gave him an incredulous stare. "And *I* happen to think it's time you *left*."

Nine

"**W**hy the hell haven't I heard from you?"

Clark held the phone away from his ear, his boss's louder-than-usual voice assaulting his ear. "Hey, man, calm down. You're liable to have a stroke."

"Sorry," Lance muttered. "It's just that I'm itching to get my hands on that property."

Clark shoved a hand through his already-disheveled hair. He had gotten out of the shower and had just sat down with a cup of coffee in hand when the phone rang. For some perverted reason he had thought it might be Sara. No such luck. Or maybe it was luck.

"You still there?"

"Yep."

"So have you made any progress at all?" Lance asked.

"Some."

"What kind of answer is that?"

Clark knew he shouldn't toy with Lance's temper like this, but since he was in such a foul mood himself, he guessed misery did indeed love company. "Actually, it's the best I have at the moment. These things take time, and you know that. For one thing, the Merricks are out of the country."

"Swell."

Clark ignored Lance's sarcasm and continued, "For another, my back's been giving me holy hell."

There was a short pause. "Tell me you're not."

"Not what?" Clark asked with drawling innocence as if he could stop the thunderburst that was about to come.

"Going to Dr. Sara Wilson for your back, dammit?"

For a moment Clark was taken aback that Lance had so quickly put two and two together. On second thought, he shouldn't have been surprised. Lance had studied the file on Sara and knew what she did for a living. And well he should have, since so much was at stake.

"I had no choice," Clark finally admitted into the stark silence.

He heard Lance's groan through the line as clearly as if he was sitting in the room with him. "Don't go off on me again, okay? If you'll just think about it, cozying up to the enemy makes sense."

"What makes you so sure she's the enemy?"

"Lots of things," Clark said, trying to curb his annoyance. Lance was just going to have to trust him.

"Which means you haven't said anything to her."

"Right. If you'll remember, you told me to check things out, make sure the timing was right."

"So you think she might give us trouble?"

"That's an understatement."

Lance cursed.

"She's proud of that facility, proud to be an owner."

"That's not what I wanted to hear."

"And her mother also lives there."

"You're really making my day," Lance said, sounding like he could bite a ten-penny nail in two.

"Under those circumstances, you'd best be glad I'm softening her up."

"As long as it's only for the good of the job," Lance said, his tone a mixture of sarcasm and humor.

Clark was glad his boss couldn't see his face. "Oh, come on, what do you take me for?"

"Just joking."

Clark shifted uncomfortably, disgusted with himself for getting into such a precarious situation.

"Have any idea how the Merricks will jump?" Lance asked.

Clark shook his head as if to clear it. "Not a clue. I've tried not to spook anyone, least of all Sara, until the Merricks return."

"Sara, huh?"

"Yes, Sara," Clark responded in a terse tone, then lightened up. "Hey, remember, I used to date her little sister."

"Ah, I see."

He didn't see, but Clark didn't give a rat. In the end Lance knew he would do what was best for the company.

"So we shouldn't expect you back in the office this week?"

"Not if you want me to see this through."

"Hell, yes. If anyone else gets wind of what we're trying to do, then we've had it. It'll turn into a blood-letting fight."

"That's not going to happen. Trust me. I'll handle it."

"That's why you're there."

"Has Phil come in?"

"As a matter of fact he just walked in my office," Lance said.

"Give him the phone."

"What's happening in the boonies?" Phil asked in his rumbling, but good-humored voice.

"Not much, but I'm working on it. Got anything for me?"

"You betcha."

"I'm all ears."

A few minutes later Clark was off the phone and sipping on his now-cold coffee. He frowned into the cup but gulped down the last swallow nonetheless.

It was after he'd gone into the kitchen and reached for the pot that he felt another sharp pain shoot through his back. He clung to the edge of the cabinet and gritted his teeth. A few seconds later he attempted to straighten.

When he was successful, he blew out a thankful breath of relief. But to hell with this. He couldn't live in fear of knocking his back out of kilter every time he so much as moved.

Maybe Sara was right. Maybe he should consider having surgery, but only if that would cure him once and for all. Until a surgeon could guarantee that outcome, he wasn't prepared to go under the knife.

Yet, feeling like he always had to walk on eggshells was for the birds.

And the pain. Even now his skin was drenched in a cold sweat. He would give anything if he were prone and Sara's hands were on him. He felt pressure that had nothing to do with his back build behind his zipper. His features darkened and an expletive flew.

He shouldn't have kissed her. That was one of the dumbest stunts he'd ever pulled. It had been a knee-jerk action, no doubt, but one he couldn't justify. He hadn't stopped mentally kicking his backside since she'd all but ordered him out of her house.

His thoughts reverted back to Lance. He had to be careful. Lance must never suspect that he had the hots for Sara Wilson. He would show no mercy. He'd not only have a verbal fit, he'd pull him off the job.

Well, the boss wouldn't know, because he intended to get himself in hand and not let it happen again. The problem was he wanted it to happen again. He had enjoyed the hell out of kissing those ripe, full lips that were so tentative at first, only to then turn as aggressive as his.

When he had pushed her away, he'd been as hard as a brick and for a little of nothing, he would have taken her right there in the vehicle which would have worsened his back.

But he hadn't been thinking about that body part. The blood pounding between his legs had taken precedence over everything else. No longer, though. It was not wise to mix business with pleasure, especially with so much at stake.

Still, he wanted to have sex with Sara Wilson. That longing had been heightened when he'd crawled into her bed and smelled the sheets.

Her smell.

He'd buried his head in the pillow and breathed deeply. Then he'd imagined her sleeping in the nude, her lithe body curled against him, her nipples poking into his back.

Crazy! That was what it was. That was what *he* was.

He had a stable of women in Houston. He could sleep with any of them at any time he wanted. That thought turned his stomach. For the moment he only wanted Sara, wanted to touch her with his hands like she'd touched him. Only he yearned to take it further; he wanted to put his mouth on her breasts.

He groaned out loud.

He had to get out of the house before he lost it.

He would go to the ranch, see Joe, then go to the nursing home and see Zelma.

Maybe he'd see Sara, as well.

"I'm leaving now, Rosa."

"It's about time. Whew! What a day."

Sara rubbed the back of her neck, then blinked her eyes, which felt like someone had thrown sand in them. She was tired. But then lack of sleep did that to her.

"Every farmer in the county must've come in today."

"I won't argue that," Sara said with a lame smile.

"If only they were as diligent about paying as they were about coming, then this clinic would be on easy street."

"Well, that's not going to happen," Sara said in a flat voice.

"Are you okay?" Rosa asked in her blunt fashion. "You seem distracted or something. You have all day."

"I'm just tired," Sara lied.

"There's nothing going on with your mom or Newt, then?"

"Not at all. Mother's feeling better than she has in a long time. And Newt," she broke off with a smile, "well, he's as cantankerous as ever."

"And as stubborn about moving."

"Absolutely. It's going to take a crane to get him out of that house."

Rosa giggled. "If anyone can bring that about, it's you."

"That remains to be seen."

"Go home and get some rest." Rosa turned the key in the front door. "Tomorrow's another day."

Although Sara left, she didn't go home. She went to Quiet Haven instead, though for a moment she considered ducking out on that responsibility for fear she would run into Clark.

Chicken!

She hadn't seen him since he'd spent the night in her bed and she'd all but ordered him out of her house for making that off-color remark, saying that he liked the way her hands felt on his flesh. Those thickly spoken words had sent her insides into a tizzy. They hadn't recovered yet.

Even though their paths hadn't crossed, Sara knew he'd been to the facility, walking very gingerly, Edwin, the administrator, had told her.

While she was glad he was finally taking an interest in his aunt, Sara was baffled as to why he was still hanging around town. With his back in the shape it was, he couldn't do much at his ranch. As far as his aunt was concerned, he'd already spent more time with her than he had in years.

She didn't get it.

More to the point, she didn't want to get it. That was the problem. This good-looking, sophisticated, *younger* man had swept into her life and turned it upside down, a fact that was both exciting and frightening.

Even if he was seriously interested in her, which he wasn't, she reminded herself with a vengeance, a relationship between them wouldn't work. The thought was ludicrous.

Discounting the obvious and troubling truth that he was five years younger than she, he was from a different world. He lived in the fast lane, while she lived in the slow one. Their personalities didn't mesh, either; they were on a collision course there, as well.

And he'd dated her sister, for Pete's sake. That stuck in her craw about as much as anything.

Still, she couldn't stop thinking about him and how his kiss had made her feel, how it had made her long for something she could never have. His attention had filled that empty cavity in her heart just enough to make it ache.

Because of that she despised him and longed for him to leave and never return. She would look after Zelma. After all, that was what she did best.

When she pulled into her parking place at Quiet Haven and saw Clark, she squeezed the steering wheel until her knuckles turned white.

"Oh, brother," she murmured, her stomach bottoming out.

He was standing just this side of one of the vegetable gardens, hoe in hand, along with one of the residents.

The "doctor" in her took precedent over everything else. She jumped out her car and made her way toward them.

"Why, hi-dee, Doc."

"Hello, Mr. Greer," Sara said, taking in the resident's wide grin that showed off nicotine-stained teeth, at least what few of them he had left. Then her gaze switched back to Clark. "What do you think you're doing?"

"Helping Sam here with his garden."

"Only he ain't much help," Sam put in.

"Are you out of your mind?" she hissed.

Clark shrugged, his eyes traveling up and down her body, his gaze deliberately mocking.

"You don't have to worry none, Doc. When it comes to digging in the dirt he's useless as tits on a boar hog."

Sara found herself relaxing as a grin tickled her lips. "Is that so, Sam?"

"Shore 'nough. That row he tried to make was as uneven as a one-legged drunk trying to walk a straight line."

"That's going to cost you big-time, Sam," Clark said, though he was grinning.

"I ain't worried."

"Well, I am," Sara said with less heat than before, reeling from seeing yet another side of this complex man. If someone had told her Clark would be in a garden fraternizing with this old man who no one cared about, she would've thought they were nuts.

"I hurt whether I'm doing anything or not," Clark said, moving to her side. When she didn't respond, he added, "God, you smell good."

Her head came up. "Don't say that."

"Why not?" he asked in a gruff voice, but for her ears alone.

"You know why not."

"Hey, sonny, git on over here, and I'll teach you how to plant 'taters the right way."

"Some other time, Sam," Clark said.

The old man's mouth turned down. "You sure?"

"Count on it." Clark smiled. "In fact, I'll take you to my ranch soon, and you can show my foreman how to start a garden."

Sam's face lit up so brightly that Sara's breath caught. Later she suspected that was why she didn't object when Clark touched her on the arm and moved her farther aside.

However, when she realized his hand remained on her, a frisson of chill bumps ran up her spine.

"Let's go," Clark said.

Sara licked her dry lips. "Where?"

"Does it matter? he asked in a thick voice, his eyes delving into hers.

Ten

"So this is the hallowed ranch."

Sara, from where she sat on the back porch of the house, took in the faraway pasturelands spotty with trees and loaded with cattle. To her right, and closer to the house, were two huge barns. This was some super place.

Clark cut her an amused glance before handing her a glass of wine he'd just brought from the kitchen. "What makes you say that?"

"It's true, isn't it?"

"Yep, guess it is, at that. So what do you think?"

"About what?" she asked with an naiveté she knew hadn't fooled him. She was right.

His smile mocked her. "The ranch, but then you knew that."

She sipped her wine, hoping its mellowness would settle her jangled nerves. She had no business being here alone with him. But when they had left Quiet Haven, she hadn't known where they were going. She hadn't really cared, either. She just wanted to be with him.

Now, though, sitting here with him in this tranquil setting, sipping on wine, terror raged inside her. She shouldn't have come. But when he had looked at her out of those smoldering eyes and spoken in that low, suggestive tone, her guard had slipped and she'd been like putty in his hands.

The thought made her want to be sick. What she should have done was insist that he take her back to her car at Quiet Haven.

She hadn't, and now she was looking trouble in the face.

"You didn't answer my question," he said, breaking into the silence.

"I've already forgotten what it was."

He threw back his head with a laugh that added to his sex appeal. Sara wanted to turn away from the picture he made dressed in jeans, boots and a white sports shirt, leaning against one of the pillars that were part of the porch.

The only thing missing was the Stetson.

"Do you like what you see, or not?"

"What's there not to like?" she said in an almost breathless voice, wondering why he cared what she thought. Perhaps he was simply making conversation. Perhaps he was as uneasy as she was. No way.

He was a man in total control of his life and his emotions.

It must be nice, she thought, suddenly wishing she could shake him up, make him lose that control.

"You can see why I'd like to eventually settle here."

"Not really," she said with more bluntness than she had intended.

Clark gave her an intense look over the rim of his glass. If she hadn't been sure her imagination was working overtime, she could've sworn his eyes lingered on her breasts before darting away. "What you're saying is that I don't fit the cowboy mode?"

His lips were twitching again as if he enjoyed this cat-and-mouse conversational foreplay. She had no objection, either, as long as the cat didn't get the better of the mouse.

"That's right."

"Which proves once again how little you know me."

"I won't argue with that."

He drained his wineglass, set it down, then concentrated on her again. "We can fix that, you know."

Sara stood, her heart starting to bang hard inside her chest. "Look, I think you'd best take me home."

"You're afraid of me, aren't you?"

His voice was low and raspy as their eyes met and held. Then Sara collected herself and lifted her chin. "Of course not."

"Then stay and let me grill you a steak."

"I'm not hungry."

''By the time it's prepared, you will be.''

Sara folded her arms across her chest. ''Do you always come on this strong?''

''Only when necessary.''

''What do you want from me, Clark?''

He didn't so much as flinch. ''For the moment just your company.'' He cocked his head and smiled. ''So how 'bout it?''

She answered his grin, feeling herself relax a bit, which she wasn't sure was a good idea. But she was tired of being so uptight. Besides, she wanted to stay. There, she had admitted it, and the truth hadn't killed her.

''Oh, all right.''

''Hey, it's a lovely evening. Actually, it's just about perfect. So what have you got to lose?''

My heart. ''I said I'd stay.''

His lips twitched. ''But not very convincingly.''

''Is there anything I can do to help with the meal?''

''Yep, fix a salad.''

''That I can do. Lead the way.''

When they had first arrived, Clark had walked her around the part of the property that he'd called his backyard before directing her onto the porch where they had been ever since.

Now, as she went inside, Sara pulled up short. While rustic and manly, it had a cozy charm all its own. ''Whoa, this is nice.''

Clark chuckled. ''You sound surprised.''

''Do I?'' Her face turned tomato-red. ''Sorry.''

His chuckle deepened. "Kind of surprises me, too, every time I walk in. That's because I can't take any of the credit. A friend's wife who's an interior designer of sorts decorated it."

"Well, I'm impressed, to say the least."

"I'm glad you like it."

Sara let that slide, knowing he was just making polite conversation. If only— Stop it! She couldn't remain sane if she allowed herself to think like that. Already she was doing herself and her emotions a grave injustice by spending leisure time with him.

Yet for the moment she was willing to let her emotions have free rein and see what happened. She had never been a chance taker or a gambler. Now she was experimenting with both and it felt damn good. Tomorrow she'd face the remnants of this evening.

"What's running through that mind of yours now?" Clark asked, standing aside for her to enter the kitchen.

"You don't want to know."

"Of course I do."

"Why are you still hanging around River Oaks?" That hadn't been what was on her mind at all. But her other thoughts were sacred and unsharable. Still, she hadn't meant to ask him such a blunt and personal question, either. It sounded like she cared.

Clark's probing blue eyes made her heart race again. "What if I said it was because of you."

Silence drummed in the room.

"I'd say you were a liar."

His eyes darkened. "Why do you sell yourself

short, Sara?'' His voice had deepened into a warm drawl. ''You're a very attractive woman.'' He paused. ''Whom I'd very much like to kiss.''

Her knees threatened to buckle under her, which made it impossible for her to move. She would like him to kiss her, too, but she couldn't allow that to happen. God only knew where another kiss would lead. Just the thought almost sent her knees to the floor. But somehow she managed to pull herself together and step back.

''I don't think that's a good idea,'' she whispered, still looking at him, helpless against the heat that flared from his eyes.

''Maybe you're right,'' he said, clearing his throat, then adding to the distance between them. ''Besides, the steaks are ready to throw on the grill.''

Sara didn't know if she was glad the spell was broken, or sad. No matter. It was for the best that things were back on a dispassionate level, a level she intended to maintain regardless of how much she wanted him to touch her.

''And I'll start the salad,'' she said in a tone that wasn't quite as breathless as before.

The pantry and refrigerator were as well stocked as the kitchen was bright and efficient. Hence, it was a pleasure to make the salad and put the potatoes on to bake.

By the time they went back out to the porch, their glasses refilled with wine, the sun was a huge ball in the sky, making its downward path between several oak trees.

The sight took Sara's breath as she sat down. "I don't think I've ever seen anything so beautiful."

"Neither have I," Clark responded, his tone low and husky.

Sara swung her head around to find his eyes on her, rather than the sunset. A flush stained her cheeks, and she wanted to lash out at him, but the words wouldn't come.

This urban cowboy was toying with her affections big-time, and she was wallowing in it like someone starving for love and attention. So why didn't she call a halt to this madness and insist he take her home? Now.

The answer was simple. Here, basking under his attention, fake or not, she could forget the loneliness that haunted her more than she wanted to admit.

"I wouldn't look at me like that if I were you, unless…" Clark let the rest of his sentence trail off, but the message was clear.

"Sorry," Sara muttered, ducking her head.

He didn't say anything else, but she felt his eyes remain on her for a few seconds before he turned his attention back to the steaks that were sizzling on the grill.

Sara longed to scrutinize him from behind, soak up every detail of his incredible physique, but she refused to indulge herself. Instead, she turned away and stared at what remained of the sunset.

"The steaks are perfect," Clark said, following a lengthy silence.

"They smell heavenly."

''I'm expecting you to eat every bite of yours.''

Sara's eyebrows lifted. "Oh, and why is that?"

"You're too thin."

Getting personal again. "That's your opinion," she said, not looking at him.

"Hey, don't get huffy. I didn't mean that the way it sounded."

She wanted to ask him exactly what he did mean, but she didn't, knowing she'd jump back into that quicksand that she'd just pulled herself out of.

The best she could hope for at this juncture was that the evening would end before she made a complete fool of herself or let him make one of her.

"Let's go chow down."

She nodded and preceded him back inside to the dining room table where they ate in between discussing the nursing home. She never tired of talking about Quiet Haven.

"You really love those old folks, don't you?" he asked, after both their plates were empty.

"Absolutely."

"And you have a wonderful way with them."

"You're not too shabby yourself," she countered softly.

He scoffed. "I don't think so."

"You had old Sam eating out of your hand."

"That was just a fluke."

It was obvious he was uncomfortable discussing himself or anything personal that might lie under that smooth facade. And that irritated her. It was almost as if he was embarrassed that she saw a softer, gentler side of him.

"So you don't intend to bring him here?"

"I said I would."

"Good, because he won't forget it."

That uneasy look remained a second longer, then his features cleared. "Let's go back on the porch and have another glass of wine."

Sara stood and instantly the room went around. "Thanks, but no thanks. I've had enough wine to last for months."

"Ah, I doubt that."

"Don't." She giggled. "Actually, I feel like my feet aren't touching the ground."

A strange light appeared in his eyes as he made his way to her side. "Oops, maybe you have had enough."

She licked her lips. "I'd...better go home."

He moved his head close to her face and whispered, "Not now."

"When?" she whispered back, swaying toward him.

He closed his arms around her. "After we make love."

Eleven

Sara blinked several times. "No."

"No?" A finger traced first the outside of her lips, then the plump, moist inside.

Again, it was all Sara could do to remain upright. "I don't think—"

"Shh, don't think." Clark's voice was thick, like he was the one who'd had too much to drink.

"Your...back," Sara began only to have her words fizzle out. He was toying with her lips again, making her ache all the way down to her toes.

"My back's fine," he said huskily, leaning just enough to replace his finger with his tongue.

Sara moaned and clung to his shirt, feeling as though she were drowning in a sea of hot passion.

She wanted this agony to come to an end. But at the same time she wanted him to continue, never to stop.

"Is that your way of saying yes?" he whispered.

He was so near her mouth now that she could smell the mellow odor of wine on his breath. "You...don't want me."

"Why would you think that?"

Even in her less-than-alert state, she heard the shock in his tone, which made her giddier.

"Of course I want you." He tightened his hold on her. "I've wanted you from the beginning."

"But I'm not beautiful," she whispered, reaching out and touching his face.

"You are to me." Without taking his eyes off her, he captured her hand in his and carried it to his mouth where he tongued her palm.

"Oh, Clark," she whispered, feeling heat rush through her body.

"Oh, Clark what?" he pressed, his tone deep and raspy.

"Kiss me."

"Then?" he prodded.

"Make...love to me." She paused with a hard swallow. "There's something you should know, something—"

He placed a finger across her lips. "I know all that's necessary for the moment."

She couldn't fight him any longer. She simply didn't have the strength to deny herself the tantalizing pleasure of his big, brawny body against her soft, pliant one.

"You have no idea how much I want you."

Following those words, he closed his mouth over hers. Instantly breaths mingled, tongues tangled and hearts pounded. Under that attack, Sara went completely limp, though her head spun.

This time the dizziness wasn't from the wine, but rather from what he was doing to her body.

His hands.

Needy hands. Knowing hands. They seemed to sense exactly where to touch to intensify that flood of heat now gathered at the apex of her thighs.

"You taste so sweet, like honey," he rasped, unbuttoning her blouse, then unclasping her bra.

Sara's eyes widened and she held her breath as a rough palm grazed across one nipple, then the other.

"Oh, Clark," she moaned again, her head going back, giving him carte blanche to her breasts.

But instead of concentrating on them, he shifted his hands to her backside, moving her ever so slowly but assuredly against his burgeoning erection.

At the brazen contact, Sara stiffened, and her next breath hung in her throat. For a moment she feared she might even choke, especially when his fingers inched underneath her panties.

She was wet. *He'd made her wet.*

When a finger found that wetness, Sara quivered.

"It's okay," he whispered, his lips nibbling on her neck. "Touch me."

"I—"

She never finished her sentence. She couldn't, not after he took her hand and placed it on his zipper.

Her hand quivered as did every nerve in her body. There was no denying he was in the same throes of agony that she was. Behind the confines of his jeans, he was hard.

"Ah, yes," he said through gritted teeth.

Then he did something she wasn't expecting. He eased two fingers inside her. "Clark!" she cried.

"Ah, so tight, so sweet," he responded in a guttural tone. "You're more than ready for me."

"Yes, oh yes!"

His fingers probed and delved. Her bones had turned to water, along with her resolve, as she sagged against him, totally at his mercy.

He kissed her again, savagely, as though *he* had reached his level of endurance, as well. While his mouth was still adhered to hers, he began to move, urging her forward with the arm that encircled her waist.

Once in the bedroom he eased her down on the bed. Without taking his hot gaze off her, he discarded her clothes, then stood and did the same thing with his own.

Sara's eyes journeyed over his body. "You're beautiful."

And he was. Although she had seen his upper torso with its hard muscles, coarse hair and tapered waist, she had purposely not let herself dwell on how he was put together below his belt.

Now she knew.

"Not nearly as beautiful as you," he whispered

into the silence, crawling onto the bed and lying beside her.

For the longest time, they stared at each other with their hearts beating out of control. Then Clark reached for her, a low growl coming from deep inside, and kissed her with a fervor that felt as it would take the the top of her head off.

He pulled away long enough to gaze deeply into her eyes again before urging her legs apart where his fingers once more found their target, probing tenderly into that wet heat.

"Ohh, Clark!" she cried again, unbelievable sensations pelting her body.

He climbed over her then and replaced his fingers with his erection, only to ease himself in, then out, creating incredible friction.

"Please," she begged, reaching for him, "don't torment me any longer."

"Oh, Sara," he whispered as he thrust farther inside her.

Sara gasped.

For a moment he paused, then whispered, "Relax, baby. It's going to be all right."

He leaned over then and while still thrusting, he took an engorged nipple into his mouth and began sucking.

Sara clutched at his back, digging her nails into his flesh, feeling as if something had broken loose inside her. Clark felt it, too, she knew, as he stroked higher and faster, creating an electricity that burned them both.

Moments later their cries filled the silence, then he rolled onto his side and faced her. "Sleep now, sweet Sara."

Sara was the first to awaken to a burst of sunlight. She frowned against the unwanted intrusion, then blinked, trying to link body and mind, but with little success. Everything seemed fuzzy, as if she was in a tangled web.

Her head ached. When she tried to move, she realized her body suffered from that same malady.

Where was she? What had happened to her? Without warning the answers came, hitting her like a fast-moving train. She was in Clark's house, at his ranch, and he had made love to her throughout the night.

She groaned inwardly at the same time her eyes flew around the room. Other than for her, it was empty. Swallowing her growing panic, she raised herself onto her elbows, jerking the sheet up to her neck, covering her naked body.

If the panic hadn't consumed her, she would have laughed. It was too late to worry about hiding her nudity. There hadn't been one crevice of her body that Clark hadn't explored with his lips, tongue and hands.

Sara's face colored as she plopped her head back on the pillow. Where was he? No sound came from any other part of the house. Had he left? Of course he hadn't, she assured herself.

Trying to control her rapidly rising heartbeat, she closed her eyes and took long, deep breaths, fearing she was going to hyperventilate if she didn't watch it.

But how could she watch it when she was at a loss as to what to do? How was she to cope with this new emotional upheaval in her life?

Clark.

In a matter of days, he had managed to turn her into another person altogether, someone she no longer recognized or knew how to deal with. Would her own mother even recognize her?

She had to get a grip on her splattered emotions. She tried, but couldn't. Her heart continued to thud, and she had a hollow feeling deep down in her stomach, like everything inside had been scooped out.

The worst part was that once she had experienced his touch, she didn't want it to end. Meaning? She swallowed against the bile that rose up the back of her throat at the same time that tears filled her eyes.

Did she love him?

Yes. But since that love was not reciprocated, she couldn't let it tarnish her life, make her bitter. It was bad enough that she was, and would remain, an old maid, but to be a *discontented* old maid would be unbearable.

She couldn't let Clark use her for his own needs, either, not when he had every intention of leaving town. The not-so-pretty truth hit her like another oncoming train—while he *was* in town, she had become his plaything.

Sara's stomach heaved, and she thought she might

be sick. But then she regained control and knew she had to get up and get dressed.

After looking at her watch, she realized she didn't have all that much time to spare before she had to be in the office.

As far as she knew, Clark didn't have one damn thing to do. Blinking back the tears, Sara got up and, dragging the sheet with her as a cover, walked to the window.

He was the first thing she saw. Clark was leaning against the fence bordering the pasture nearest the house. Was he thinking about her?

Probably.

But not with love in his heart, she reminded herself. Still, she had no regrets, though she sensed he did, if the dejected set of his shoulders was anything to judge by.

Sighing, Sara turned from the window and was about to reach for her clothes when she heard the sound. A phone. Then it dawned on her; her cell was ringing.

Where was it? Fear filled every corner of her mind. Katherine. Had something happened to her mother? No one ever called her on that phone unless it was an emergency, because she always wore her pager. Hysterical laughter erupted. No pagers allowed on a naked body.

Clasping her hand on her mouth to curb her hysterics, she scanned the premises. Her purse was lying on the only chair in the room.

Clark must have brought it in before he left.

Yanking the sheet upward, Sara closed the distance between her and the shoulder bag. By the time she got the damn phone out and said hello, her breathing was coming in spurts.

"Sara?"

It was Edwin. Oh, God, it was her mother. On top of everything else, she couldn't handle that. She gripped the tiny gadget so tightly that she feared she'd crack her hand.

"I'm here," she croaked, unable to ask what was wrong.

"This concerns you, too, but it's Clark Garrison I'm trying to reach."

"Er…what makes you think I know where he is?"

"I don't. I was just hoping."

"What's going on?"

"Zelma's missing."

It took a few seconds for his words to soak in. "You mean, she's gone?"

"Yes, I'm sorry to say. We can't find her anywhere."

Twelve

A virgin.

He still couldn't believe Sara had never been with a man. Clark shoved back his Stetson, then slapped his forehead in frustration as he continued to use the fence post for a prop.

Although his eyes were on the dew-covered grass that sparkled like it had been sprinkled with millions of diamonds, his mind was in turmoil.

Oh, he had suspected that Sara was naive in many ways. Her quiet and unassuming demeanor had been the first clue. And the fact that she wasn't married at thirty-nine had been another. Yet the flip side of that coin was that she could've had sundry affairs.

Only she hadn't.

So what was the next step for him? His emotions were in shreds. On the one hand, he felt humbled to have been the first to introduce her to the world of sexual passion.

On the other, he was mortified at the responsibility such an act carried. He knew Sara wasn't the one-night-stand type. But he was. Actually, that was all he had to offer.

He didn't want to become emotionally involved with another woman, certainly not one whose lifestyle and goals were so different from his. Hell, the bottom line was he didn't want to get *married* again. He'd been down that road and had ended up in a ditch.

Now, if Sara would agree to live with him, that would be a different matter altogether. He could go for that real easily. But that wasn't about to happen, not as long as her mother was alive.

Yet he didn't want to stop seeing her. He couldn't imagine not being able to *touch* her whenever he wanted to. Even now, after hours of making love, of pleasing her and teaching her to please him, Clark felt himself grow hard again.

Muttering a foul word, he shifted uncomfortably.

Maybe it was that innocence, that sweetness, that had him by the throat. A smile that was short on humor flexed his drawn lips.

Sweet?

Who was he trying to kid? She'd been anything but sweet once she'd learned that his body was her play toy, that she could do anything she damned well wanted to.

He squirmed against the onslaught of passion that almost sent him flying back up the hill, into the house and into the bed. He suspected she was sleeping. He could picture her in his mind's eye—her hair all mussed from rolling and tumbling, her lips red and swollen like a ripe strawberry from having been kissed so much.

And her body—open and inviting to his fingers and mouth.

Clark banged a hand against the post, then yelped, "Son of a—!"

However much he'd hoped physical pain would take his mind off his mental anguish, it didn't. No doubt the fire he had awakened in Sara had burned him badly. He wanted her more than he'd ever wanted any woman, including his ex-wife.

The kicker was he'd been happier and more contented these past few days than ever in his life, which surprised him. Still, he wasn't in love, nor was he ready to retire and live here.

Why, he'd wither and die on the vine in this town right now. Hell, he liked the bright lights. He liked to be around the movers and shakers—people like him. He couldn't imagine awakening every morning to the sound of crickets instead of cars.

But whether he wanted to admit it or not, getting off the fast track and onto the slow one had made a marked difference in him. It had smoothed the wrinkles in his face and soothed the acid in his gut. With the exception of his back, he'd felt better than he had in a long time.

To some extent even the nursing home had played its part in calming him. He had really enjoyed seeing and spending time with his aunt Zelma, Katherine and old Sam.

Old Sam. He chuckled to himself, thinking about the elderly gentleman. Then his smile faded as he remembered that Sam had no one who cared a tinker's damn about him. And he'd promised to bring him to the ranch.

Clark shook his head in disgust. That kind of sentimental crap messing with his head would accomplish nothing except get him in trouble, not only with himself but with his boss.

Thinking of Lance filled him with a pang of guilt. Instead of making love to Sara, he should've been making a deal. He figured Lance's patience was soon going to come to an end.

''Mornin', boss.''

At the sound of Joe's voice, Clark whipped around. His foreman was frowning up at him, his grungy hat kicked back on his head.

''Wasn't expecting to see you here,'' Joe said. ''Anything going on?''

Clark could read the puzzlement in Joe's eyes, hear it in his voice, but he wasn't about to give him an explanation. ''Nah, I spent the night, that's all.''

''I'm bettin' you slept like a baby, too.''

Wrong. He hadn't slept at all. ''The air does feel different,'' Clark responded in a lame voice.

"Are you gonna be around for a while?" Joe asked.

"Nope. Not today. I've got work to do."

Joe was quiet for a moment, then asked, "Is something wrong?"

"What makes you think that?"

"Dunno. You just look like someone gutted you."

Clark smothered an expletive. Was he wearing his feelings on his shoulder for all to see? If so, he'd best get his act together. Now.

"I just have a lot on my mind. That's all."

"Clark!"

The sound of Sara's voice turned both men's heads toward the house just in time to see her step off the porch and wave to Clark.

"Mmm," Joe said, rubbing his chin as he cut Clark a sly look. "Now that's something mighty nice to have on your mind."

"It's not what you think," Clark said gruffly.

Joe grinned. "Whatever you say."

"Clark, hurry!"

His heart skipped a beat. Sara? Was she hurt? He didn't think so. At least she appeared all right. But then he wasn't that close.

"Not one word to anybody, you hear?" Clark threw back at Joe, his eyes narrowed.

Joe held up both hands, a bland look on his face. "I ain't seen nothing or nobody."

"Thanks," Clark muttered, then turned and started up the hill, unable to move as fast as he would've liked because of his back.

As if Sara realized that, she came running to him. By the time they met, his breathing was as rapid as hers.

Something bad *had* definitely happened.

"You're kiddin' me," Clark said.

"I don't kid about things like that," Sara said, her tone huffy.

"We'll find her."

Sara went limp with relief, having expected Clark to go ballistic when she'd told him that Zelma was missing.

"But I still don't understand how that could've happened."

"Unfortunately, it happens," Sara responded, "or so I understand from administrators in other nursing homes."

Clark blew out his breath, then raked his gaze over her, a smoldering, intimate gaze that left no doubt he had switched his thoughts and was now thinking about what had taken place between them.

Flushing, Sara turned away.

"Don't," he said huskily.

She swung back around. "Don't what?"

"Don't *not* look at me."

Sara almost smiled, but her mouth couldn't quite complete that simple gesture. It was as if her face and her body were frozen. "I—"

"Do you hate me?"

Her flush deepened. "Why would you think that?"

"Dammit, Sara, why didn't you tell me—" He broke off as if he'd choke on the word *virgin.*

Every nerve in her rebelled, but she didn't let it show. "Look, now's not the time to discuss us. Discuss *that.*"

Her voice was cool and detached. Her worst fear had come about. He was sorry he'd made love to her, and she knew why. Since he'd taken her virginity, he was afraid she'd want more than he was willing to give.

"But just to put your mind at ease, I don't expect you to marry me." She couldn't hide the sarcasm that colored her voice.

"Dammit, Sara, that—"

"Later." Her voice was cold. "I don't want to talk about us. Getting to the nursing home and finding your aunt should be all that's on our minds."

Although he didn't push the subject, she knew he wasn't happy. He sat grimly behind the wheel while she kept her eyes straight ahead. Not another word passed between them, but the tension danced around them like lightening crackling on the stormiest of days.

When they arrived at the facility, that tension remained. She was still dodging Clark's probing gaze while she went about the business at hand.

The staff had tried to keep Zelma's disappearance under wraps, to keep from upsetting the other residents. So far, their determination had paid off. The day was progressing as usual.

Sara had told her mother. While Katherine had

been visibly shaken, she'd been positive and supportive which had made Sara feel much better.

However, she couldn't hide her growing concern. "I can't believe this happened," she muttered more to herself than to anyone else.

Sara tried to keep her voice even, but she heard the trembling fear in it and knew that the others heard it as well. But then she wasn't the only one who was feeling frantic.

Edwin Turner, who had shaken hands with Clark for the first time, looked like someone had sucker punched him in the stomach. And Clark's face—she sneaked a glance at him—looked cast out of steel.

But it was Dottie Meyers, the nurse on duty at the time, who was bearing the brunt of Zelma's disappearance. Underneath her fairly calm veneer, Sara sensed she was close to hysterics.

No patient had ever walked off from the facility. Ever. Until now. Until Zelma. Of course, the sheriff had been called, and his men were combing the area. So far they had turned up nothing, which was both good and bad.

"Where could she be?" Dottie cried for the umpteenth time.

Sara patted her on the shoulder. "We'll find her."

"But what if she's—" Dottie's voice faded into nothing as if she couldn't go on, as if the thought was too horrible to put into words.

"If someone picked her up," Clark said in taut voice, "then maybe the cops can find an eye witness."

"I'm so sorry, sir, about this," Edwin said to Clark. "I take full responsibility."

Clark shook his head. "I'm not blaming you or anyone else. With Alzheimer's patients, it's a crap shoot as to what's going through their minds."

"Mr. Garrison," Edwin said, "after giving this some thought, do you have any idea where she could've gone?"

Sara watched Clark and saw the grimness painted on his face. He didn't have a clue as to where Zelma might be. Since he'd left town years ago, he didn't have a clue about his aunt, period.

As if he sensed her censure, Clark rested his eyes on Sara for another brief moment, his features hardening that much more.

"No," he said tersely.

"Let's try the house one more time," Sara said.

All three looked at her.

"But why?" Edwin asked. "A deputy's been by there several times already."

Sara shrugged. "I know, but humor me."

"I'll take her," Clark said. "Come on."

Edwin spread his hands. "Keep me posted, and I'll do the same."

The drive to Clark's old stomping grounds was also done in silence. Sara purposely kept her face glued to the window, discouraging conversation, personal or otherwise.

But she was stewing inside. If word got out what had happened, loved ones would be leery of placing their family members at Quiet Haven, which spelled *doom* in bold, capital letters.

More than the home's reputation, she was so worried about Zelma. God love her, she was vulnerable as a newborn baby. Sara couldn't bear to think about the horrific things that could befall that defenseless old woman.

"It's not your fault, you know," Clark said into the silence.

"Oh, but it is," Sara shot back. "As an owner, I'm responsible for the welfare of the residents."

"I think you're being too hard on yourself."

"That's because you don't know anything about the nursing home business."

He didn't say anything.

"It's about people and taking care of them."

"I understand that."

"Somehow, I don't think you do." She averted her gaze again, but not before she saw his face drain of color and his grip tighten on the steering wheel.

She'd pissed him off, but that couldn't be helped.

"Well, I'll be damned."

"What?" she asked as Clark pulled the UV to a stop in front of the house. Then she knew. "Oh, my God."

Zelma was sitting in the porch swing, her neighbor Daisy Floyd by her side.

"I should've known," Clark muttered.

Sara paid his muttering no heed as she jumped out and dashed up the steps. "Thank God, you're all right, Zelma."

"Why wouldn't she be, Doc?" Daisy asked. "I was taking care of her."

Sara turned around and faced Clark. They merely looked at each other, then burst out laughing.

"So what now?" Clark asked.

"I'm going to the office," Sara responded with force. "I have patients waiting, or at least I hope so."

Zelma had been delivered back to the facility, and things had settled down, though not before she and Clark had had a "come to Jesus meeting" with Daisy, who had somehow managed to walk into the facility, then walk out with Zelma.

"Zelma told me she wanted to come home, so I brought her," Daisy had said.

Sara had thought Clark was going to have a stroke, but he'd kept his cool and his mouth shut, letting her deal with the problem.

"It's our time to talk now," Clark said, interrupting her thoughts and bringing her back to reality.

"No, it isn't."

"Yes, it is."

Without answering, Sara turned. He grabbed her arm, stopping her. Slowly she lifted her eyes to his, then back down to where his big hand surrounded her flesh. "Let go of me."

"I'm not going away, Sara. Count on it."

She got into her car, cranked it, then drove off, her heart in her throat.

Thirteen

She wasn't mad at him. She was mad at herself. Damn, damn, damn, Sara fumed, pacing back and forth across the carpet in her bedroom.

Once she had arrived home from the hair-raising escapade with Zelma, she had showered, dressed and was finally ready to go to the clinic. She had checked with Rosa and found out she didn't have anything to worry about as far as her appointments were concerned. None were scheduled until after lunch. But that time was fast approaching, Sara noticed, glancing at the clock on her bedside table.

Be that as it may, she wasn't in any condition emotionally or mentally to see patients. She didn't know what she was going to do about Clark. What if he left today, went back to Houston, just like that?

Sara's heart almost stopped along with her legs. She grabbed the back of the dressing table chair for support. If he drove out of town right now, she would have no one to blame but herself. After all, he'd tried to talk to her. But no, she'd behaved like an outraged virgin who had been taken advantage of.

Her bitter laugh bounced off the walls, giving the room a hollow sound, much like her insides felt. She had elicited everything he did to her, from the first kiss to the last one, and most certainly *everything* in between.

Thinking once again about what she had let him do to her body, and what she had done to his in return, scorched her face. A hand flew up to one cheek. It even felt hot to the touch. Dropping her hand, she shoved it into her pocket, then bit down on her lower lip.

That was when she peered in the mirror. Did she look any different? This was the first time she'd actually had the chance to give herself the once-over for overt signs of someone who had just lost her virginity.

Another burst of laughter erupted, then Sara sobered, inching closer to her image. Nope. No telltale signs that she'd made love all night, except that maybe her lips were redder and plumper than usual.

Her tall, willowy frame hadn't changed, nor had her auburn-colored hair or her vivid green eyes. The only thing that might give her away was the heightened color on her cheeks. No matter how much powder she had put on, and it had been a lot, her skin refused to fade.

Realizing she was acting like an idiot, Sara whipped around, grabbed her purse and headed toward the door. If and when she got the chance, she wouldn't shy away from Clark. Maybe his intentions were honest after all.

She smiled at such a silly notion. However, it gave her the courage to leave the room and face the day. Her hand was on the front doorknob when the phone rang.

Should she ignore it? More than likely it was Rosa calling wanting to know where she was. But what if it was Clark? Now that she'd kicked her rear sufficiently, she wanted desperately to hear his voice.

Dropping her bag, Sara crossed to the secretary in one corner of the room and reached for the phone.

The calling party wasn't Clark, but rather her old boss in Dallas, Alfred Noble.

"Well, I thought you'd forgotten all about me," Sara said in a lighthearted tone.

"You know better than that."

Alf was one of her favorite people. Like Newt, he was up in years and just as blunt and crusty. He even looked a little like Newt with his tall, lanky body and thick gray hair. Unlike Newt, he was a still-practicing, crackerjack chiropractor.

"So how are things in Big D?" she asked.

"We're up to our elbows in patients," he said without preamble.

"You sound like that's a bad thing." Sara sighed

inwardly. She'd give her eye-teeth to be in that position.

"It's just hectic. How are things in your neck of the woods?"

"Well, I'm not even up to my *knees* in patients."

Alf laughed loud enough that she had to hold the receiver away from her ear. "Then come back."

"Excuse me?"

"You heard what I said."

"Are you serious?"

"Hell, yes, I'm serious. I've been meaning to call you for weeks now and haven't had the time. You can name your own price and your own days, down to the minutes, if you've a mind to."

"I don't know quite what to say, Alf."

"Just say yes and be done with it."

"You know it's not that easy."

"Is your mother okay?"

"Yes."

"And you're okay?"

Sara chuckled. "Yes, Alf."

"And you still have that note on the nursing home?"

"Ohhh, yes."

"So you don't have any reason to say no. Hell, three days a week here would be a godsend for both of us."

Sara shook her head, trying to absorb into her thick skull what this could mean. But now wasn't the right time.

"Look, Alf, let me mull this over, talk to Mother. I'll get back to you."

"Make it soon, honey. This clinic hasn't been the same since you left."

"Thanks. I've sure missed you stroking my ego."

"What ego?" Alf threw back just before she heard a dial tone.

Moments later Sara dashed out the door. *Whew, what else was going to happen?*

Two days later she still hadn't heard from Clark nor had she made up her mind about Alf's offer. She had visited with her mother at length about the job, but she hadn't mentioned her torrid night with Clark. And she wouldn't, of course.

She was aching inside, on both accounts. While she knew returning to Dallas for three days a week would go a long way in pulling her out of her financial hole, she didn't want to leave the peace and tranquility of River Oaks.

Moving back to the city would entail uprooting her life again, actually living two separate lives. She couldn't commute; it was too far, which meant she would have to find an apartment somewhere close to the clinic. And that drive. She hated being on the road, back and forth.

The bottom line was that she didn't want to do that unless she absolutely had to. Right now she still had some savings to draw from. Still, she couldn't just blow off the opportunity. For the future of the nursing facility, she had to consider taking it.

As far as not having heard from Clark—well, she didn't blame him. Yet his absence hurt, and there was no medicine on earth that would help or heal a heartache.

Had he gone back to Houston without so much as a word? She couldn't bear that thought, but she just might have to.

Suddenly the doorbell rang, jarring her out of her tormenting thoughts. Clark. Oh, Lord, let it be Clark, but only if he was upright and healthy. She didn't want him coming to see her because his back was bothering him.

What if that was why she hadn't seen him? Maybe she should check on him tomorrow. Maybe he was down and couldn't get up.

Rubbish.

Sara all but raced to the door and flung it open, only to have her jaw follow suit.

"Hello, sister, dear."

"Alice?"

"Close your mouth," her sibling said, picking up the luggage at her feet, then breezing by Sara into the living room.

Sara closed the door and joined her. "What on earth is going on?"

Alice shrugged before plopping down on the couch. "Same ole, same ole. Dennis and I are having problems."

"Meaning?" Sara had to ask, but she dreaded hearing the answer. The last thing she needed was her little sister landing on her doorstep.

"Meaning I'm putting some much-needed space between us."

Sara sat down on the other end of the sofa, realizing her legs were shaking. "So you haven't left him, as in getting a divorce?"

"Not yet, anyway."

Alice and her high-and-mighty lawyer husband had been having marital problems off and on for years, problems that Sara had been privy to via long-distance telephone. Even so, she never expected Alice to walk out on Dennis.

"Where are the kids?" Sara asked, unable to believe that Alice would leave them, as well. Her sister might be flighty and spoiled, but she couldn't imagine her deserting her children.

"They're on a week's camping trip with friends."

"Well, Mother'll be disappointed that she didn't get to see them, but she'll be ecstatic that you're home."

"Is Mom really doing okay?" Alice asked, running a hand through her long, blond hair and ruffling it.

"She's great, actually."

Sara had tried so hard not to envy her sister anything, but somehow her efforts always fell short. Alice, after marrying and having two children, still had an hourglass figure, not to mention a glorious abundance of blond hair, wonderful skin and clear blue eyes. And she had the personality to match her looks.

She had been and remained everything that Sara wasn't. Still, Sara wouldn't have traded places with her for all the tea in China. Sara doubted Alice knew the real meaning of love, except when it came to herself.

Sara battled back a sigh as she wondered what she was going to do with this unexpected added nuisance. With her own life turned topsy-turvy, she didn't need Alice to worry about.

"Tell me, Big Sis, what's been going on with you?"

"Not one thing worth talking about."

"In this dump, I don't doubt it." Alice frowned. "Why in heaven's name you ever came back beats me."

Sara stood, walked over and kissed Alice on the cheek. "You'd never understand, so don't clutter your mind. How 'bout something to eat?"

"No, thanks. I stopped on the way from the airport and grabbed a bite. I think I'll hit the sack if you don't mind. I'm pooped."

"You and me both. I have to work in the morning, but you go see Mother. I'll come as soon as I can."

"Works for me," Alice said glibly.

Sara watched her sister disappear down the hall, then she made her way into her own room. She tried to sleep, but her eyes wouldn't stay shut. Though she realized how absurd it was, she couldn't stop thinking about what would happen when Alice and Clark met again.

If Clark was still in town, and she prayed he was, then it was inevitable he would run into Alice, most likely at Quiet Haven.

Would the old sparks fly?

Sara groaned, then punched the pillow, trying to shut her mind off. It seemed as if she was hell-bent on punishing herself with thoughts of the past.

From the get-go, Alice had been crazy about Clark, the popular bad boy who could've had any girl in school, only he had chosen Alice. If her mother had approved, Sara suspected her sister might have married him. With both of them being blond and beautiful, what fine children they would've had.

That thought was so distasteful that her stomach rebelled. She punched the pillow again. Harder. Then it hit her what she was doing to herself and for no reason. Alice was already married with children, for god's sake.

Anyway, what was between Clark and Alice had been over years ago, water under the proverbial bridge, muddy water, at that. Still, and crazy as it was, Sara dreaded for them to meet, knowing that it was nothing but pure jealousy that fueled that feeling.

That thought was still uppermost in her mind the following morning when she walked into the clinic, looking and feeling like hell.

"Did you by chance tie one on last night?" Rosa asked.

Rosa's eyes held a teasing glint, but Sara knew that was her nurse's way of asking what was wrong.

"I wish."

"Wanna talk about it?"

"My sister showed up on my doorstep."

That explanation was far from the whole truth, but that was all Sara was prepared to share.

Rosa's big eyes turned bigger. "You mean to stay?"

"Let us pray not."

"Oh, dear," Rosa said, shaking her head.

"You got it." Sara's tone was bleak. "Enough about my personal problems. We have some patients waiting."

And boy was she glad. Anything that would consume her mind, take it off herself, was a blessing.

She walked into the room with a smile on her face. "Ah, Mr. Franks, what have we here?"

"Nothin' I hope, but the old lady said I'd better come, or else."

Sara smiled. "I guess we'd better take a look-see, then."

The hands on the clock registered two before she finished with her work for the day and walked into Quiet Haven.

Edwin was the first person she saw. She smiled and asked, "How's the day going?"

He rolled his eyes. "Without mishap, thank God."

"I second that."

Sara left him with those words and headed to her mother's room. The door was open, and what she saw brought her up short.

Clark was in the process of getting to his feet. When he did, his big body seemed to shrink the small room even more. For a moment their eyes met. But Sara couldn't read a damn thing in his.

"Hey, Sis, stop hovering at the door and come on in," Alice said.

Sara forced a smile, though she sensed it was a brittle one at best.

"Hi, darling," Katherine said. "It's about time you got here."

"I have to work, you know," Sara said in a light voice, though her heart was beating far too fast. Clark's presence had thrown her insides into chaos.

"Isn't it wonderful your sister's here?"

Sara leaned over and kissed her mother on the cheek. "That goes without saying."

"And Clark, too, of course," Katherine added with an extra glow in her cheeks.

"Of course," Sara responded in what she prayed was a normal tone, not daring to look at him again. "So what's going on?"

"Clark and I were catching up on old times."

Sara's nightmare had turned into reality just as she had feared. But she would die before she'd let anyone know what was going through her mind.

"Oh, really?" Sara flashed a bright smile at no one in particular.

"Yep." Alice grinned.

"Actually, it's your sister who's done most of the catching up."

"I'll second that," Katherine said, her smile looking fixed on her face.

"Which is all the more reason why we should

have dinner tonight at one of our old hangouts,'' Alice said, batting her eyes. "That way *you* can fill me in on what's happening with you.''

In the sudden and heavy silence that descended on the room, her mother's knitting needles clicking together sounded like gunfire.

Sara forced herself to look at Clark who seemed perfectly at ease except for one thing, a nerve bunched in his jaw.

"So are you going?'' Sara asked, forcing another smile, though she was unraveling on the insides faster than her mother's yarn.

Alice cut her eyes to Sara, then back to Clark. "Of course he's going.''

Fourteen

―――

"Uncle Newt, what is there about you that makes me feel better?"

"My charm."

Sara grinned. "Now, why didn't I figure that out?"

Newton harrumphed.

"I'm serious, Uncle Newt. Coming here does work some kind of magic on me."

"I don't know how or why. Hell, I still don't know what has you so upset."

"Just chalk it up to PMS," Sara lied with a smile.

"You won't talk because you think I'm sick."

"You're not as sick as you are ornery."

"I know when this old ticker needs special attention,'' he said, patting his chest, "as well as these old bones. So will you please stop worrying.''

"No, but for now, you're the boss."

"Then tell me what has you looking like you've been drawn and quartered.''

"Thanks, Uncle Newt," Sara said with a downward twist of her mouth.

"Well, it's the truth, and you know it.''

"I already feel better, really. Just seeing your sweet old face did the trick.''

Newton rolled his eyes. "Women!''

Sara leaned over and gave him a warm kiss on the cheek, then headed for the door. "Have you given any more thought to moving into Quiet Haven?''

Newt's facial expression turned into a scowl. "I'll make a deal with you. The day I can't take care of myself, that's the day you can haul me off to that adult playpen.''

Sara merely shook head. "No deal, you old coot. I want you to go now, before that happens.''

"I'm not budging.''

Sara blew him a kiss, then said in a sugary tone, "We'll see.''

By the time she walked into her house a few minutes later, Sara's false bravado that she had clung to while at Newton's had disappeared, though she had gone there with every intention of venting her frustrations on him.

But it hadn't worked out that way. She had taken one look at him and known he wasn't feeling up to par. His color was bad, and he seemed to have lost more weight. Somehow she had to get him out of that house and into the assisted-living facility. She just wished he weren't so stubborn.

Besides, she had no business burdening him with her troubles. She had to stop that, especially when it came to Clark. But the thought of him with her sister was almost more than she could stand. Hence, she tried not to think about it.

She had gone to bed long before Alice had gotten in last night, and left before she awakened. She hadn't wanted to know one thing about their dinner. It would hurt too much.

"Sara, is that you?"

Alice's hyper and unexpected voice froze Sara in place. She had hoped her sister wouldn't be there, that she'd still be at the nursing home. It had been a long day, and Sara coveted a hot bath and some time alone to think.

She hadn't been that busy at the clinic, but she'd been too fretful to concentrate, especially with Rosa in and out like a busy bee.

"Of course it's me." Sara stiffened. "Who else were you expecting?" If she said Clark, Sara swore she'd belt her one. Then she felt terrible at such a thought.

But dammit, he's mine!

Alice already had a husband and two beautiful children. Sara's eyes filled with tears. Fearing Alice would see her crying, Sara scrambled in her purse for a tissue. She had just wiped them away when Alice strode into the living room.

"Hi-ya."

Sara half smiled as she pitched her carryall and purse on the sofa. "I figured you'd be with Mother." *Or Clark.*

"I have been," Alice said with a smile.

"She's okay." It wasn't a question but a flat statement of fact for lack of anything better to say. Dammit, but she felt uncomfortable around her own sister, which was nothing new, Sara reminded herself.

Now, however, that feeling was exacerbated. Jealousy. It gnawed at her insides. If Alice had encouraged Clark to kiss—

"You're mad at me, aren't you?" Alice asked out of the blue, though with her winsome smile intact.

Sara ignored that smile by averting her head. She didn't want Alice to see the color that flooded her cheeks. "Why on earth would you think that?"

"Before we get into any heavy discussion, how 'bout some iced tea?"

Jolted by the sudden change of subject, Sara faced Alice again, her eyebrows raised.

Alice nodded toward the kitchen. "I just made a fresh pitcher."

"Thanks, I'd love some." Sara strove to loosen up and put some warmth back into her voice, but it was hard. For one thing, she was shocked that Alice had lifted a finger in the kitchen. She'd always expected someone to wait on her, instead of the other way around.

For another, she didn't want to have a "heavy discussion" as Alice had phrased it. She simply wanted to be alone to nurse her misery. More to the point, she didn't want to be with the person who was partly responsible for that misery.

"Here, drink up," Alice said, waltzing back into the room and handing her the drink.

"Thanks," Sara muttered, sitting on the sofa where she kicked her shoes off and tucked her feet under her.

Alice sat in an adjacent chair, then took a big gulp of her tea. "You look beat."

"I am beat," Sara said flatly.

Alice flushed, though her chin jutted. "You don't have to bite my head off."

"Look, Alice, you're my sister, and I'm glad you're here, but—"

"You don't want me messing around with Clark, right?"

Anger prickled down the back of her neck and spine, but Sara kept her voice as nonchalant and generic as possible. "What possessed you to say a thing like that?"

"I saw the way you looked at him yesterday in Mother's room."

"That's ridiculous."

Alice took another sip of her tea, though her gaze never wavered. Sara cringed, fighting the urge to bolt. If Alice had read her facial expression, did that mean Clark had, too?

That thought made her crazy.

"Oh, I don't think it's ridiculous at all," Alice countered in a soft, sweet tone.

Sara gave Alice an incredulous stare. Was this her spoiled sibling acting as if she cared? Where was that underlying cattiness in her tone?

"Look, Alice, I'd rather not talk about Clark."

She might not have spoken for all the attention Alice paid her comment. "I know you were upset that we went to dinner last night."

"Again, I'd rather not—"

"Hear me out, okay, then you can tell me to go butt a stump, if you still want to."

Sara pursed her lips, readying herself for the humiliation that was sure to follow.

"While Mother and I both would love for you to find a man to love you, Clark's not him."

Sara took a deep breath and counted to ten, while keeping her face devoid of any expression. She hated being lectured by her younger sister, whether it was well intended or not. Hell, she knew Clark wasn't for her. She certainly didn't need anyone to confirm that.

"I'm well aware of that, Alice."

"Please, don't be mad at me for saying that. I'm just concerned, that's all."

Sara released a pent-up sigh. "I know, but you have enough on your own plate without adding anything of mine to it."

For a moment Alice looked a bit disconcerted. Sara knew her words had hit their mark.

"You're right," Alice said in an unabashed tone, "but again, I just don't want to see you get hurt."

A shadow of a smile touched Sara's lips. "I'm a big girl, in case you've forgotten."

"I know, but you're naive as hell, too."

Sara took umbrage with that. "That's my problem, not yours."

"God, you're stubborn as a mule," Alice said. "Clark and I had dinner just for old times' sake, nothing more, nothing less."

"So, I'm glad."

"Dammit, Sara, I know there's something going on between you two."

"Did he say that?" Sara heard the catch in her voice, but couldn't do anything about it.

"He just told me that you'd worked on his back a couple of times and that you had magic fingers."

Sara's face turned scarlet, something else she couldn't do anything about. "I'm glad I was able to help him."

"He has no intention of hanging around here, you know."

"Did he tell you that?"

"Not in so many words, but he didn't have to."

"I see."

"No, Sara, I don't think you do. He's a ladies' man, always has been and always will be. One woman will never be able to satisfy him."

Sara felt her heart crack another degree. "I'll keep that in mind," she said lightly, then stood.

Alice peered up at her. "I hope you will, for your own protection, if nothing else."

"I'm going to take a bath and hit the sack."

"Me, too."

Sara paused. "How 'bout you and Dennis?"

"Having had dinner with Clark seems to have put things in perspective for me." Alice gave a woeful smile. "Does that sound crazy?"

"Not if it works," Sara responded, a real warmth in her tone this time. "So what are you going to do?"

"Go home tomorrow, after I tell Mother."

Sara hugged her. "I hope everything works out. I'll keep my fingers crossed."

"Please do, and thanks for putting up with me."

An awkward moment passed, then Sara added, "Anytime. And good luck."

"Sleep tight, Sis."

Fat chance, she thought.

Sara was right. She and the pillow fought all night. Memories of Clark and how he'd made her feel when he had thrust high and hard inside her haunted her.

Finally the sun peered through the window. All Sara had to show for having gone to bed was a pillow drenched with tears.

Clark realized Sara was pissed off at him for more reasons than one. First off, he had avoided her for two days after having made love to her. Second, he'd gone to dinner with her sister.

But hell, in defense of himself, he had done what he'd thought was best by disappearing. Too, he had tried to talk to her and she wouldn't listen.

As for the dinner with Alice, he'd been railroaded into that, pure and simple. He'd wanted to say no outright. But under the circumstances he hadn't wantcd to cmbarrass anyone or make a big deal out of the invitation.

Yet hc'd cnjoycd the evening because Alice hadn't thrown herself at him as he'd suspected she might. He flushed at the size of his ego, but what else was he to have thought? Alice used to come on to him like gangbusters.

But to his surprise and delight, she had talked about her kids and husband nonstop. While he'd listened, or hoped he had, his mind had been on Sara and how she'd looked when Alice had announced they were going to dinner.

Fragile.

That had been the word that jumped to mind. She had looked as though a light puff of wind could've knocked her off her feet. So what did that mean? Did she care about him?

So what if she did?

That wouldn't change anything. He cared about her, as well, but not enough to stroll down the aisle. Yet he had no intention of leaving Sara alone. Right now he wanted to make love to her so badly he was in a world of hurt. But unfortunately his lust would have to take second place to his work, at least for the moment.

He had learned at the gas station, from the chatty attendant, that the Merricks were back in town. He'd come straight to his aunt's house and called them.

They agreed to meet with him, though they had seemed perplexed by his request. Of course, he hadn't volunteered any information. That type of business was not something one discussed on the phone.

Next he'd picked up the phone and called Edwin Turner, Quiet Haven's administrator, who had also agreed to meet with him.

"I hope this is not about Zelma."

Before Clark could say anything, Edwin went on, "I'd hate to see you take her out because of that one terrible episode."

"I have no intention of taking her out of the facility."

"Oh, then what do you want to see me about?"

Clark hesitated, then decided Edwin's point-blank question demanded the same kind of answer. "I'm interested in buying Quiet Haven."

A dead silence followed his words.

"Mr. Turner?"

"Er, I'm still here. You'll have to forgive me, but you took me totally by surprise."

"That's understandable."

"Have you spoken with the owners yet?"

"No, but I intend to. However, that's between us for now."

Edwin didn't say anything.

"So, I'll see you at the appointed time."

"Fine."

Once the phone was back in the cradle, he rubbed the back of his neck.

Clark's conscience pricked him. He should call Sara and invite her to the meeting with the Merricks. In fact, he felt like a heel for not doing so.

But he couldn't. When he told Sara, he wanted to do it alone, just the two of them. Still, it wouldn't be a fun time. Her answer would be an emphatic no, even though she was in deep financial straits.

However, if the Merricks were in his corner, she wouldn't have much choice since she owned only one-third of Quiet Haven, leaving the Merricks with the majority. But forcing her signature on the dotted line left a bad taste in Clark's mouth, something he'd never had a problem with in the past.

Regardless, he was determined to see this deal through, reminding himself once again that buying and selling nursing homes for profit was his job, and a lucrative one at that.

So why did thoughts of hurting Sara keep intruding?

Clark lurched across the room only to grab his back, feeling as if someone had hit him there with a doubled-up fist. "Damn!"

Well, he'd been looking for an excuse to see Sara. Now he had one. Both his back and his loins were in dire need of her undivided attention.

Fifteen

———

"Are you sure I'm not in heaven?"

"I'm sure," Sara said tartly, pressing a little harder on his back than she should have.

Clark groaned.

"Sorry," Sara murmured, contrite. He knew exactly which buttons to push and she had let him.

When he had shown up at the end of the workday without an appointment, Rosa had let him waltz right into her office as if he had a right to be there. She didn't blame Rosa. Clark could charm even the hardest of hearts. He'd charmed hers, and she had thought she was immune.

Ha!

"How do you feel now?" Sara asked, removing

her hands before she found herself stroking instead of massaging.

"A little better."

In spite of herself, she smiled. "Then consider this session over."

"Boy, was my time in heaven short-lived."

"Consider yourself lucky you even got there."

Clark twisted his head up and around, then grinned. "You're mad."

Sara tried not to blush, but her efforts failed. "Now, why on earth would I be mad at you?" She hoped her nonchalant attitude fared better than her face. It was a dead giveaway.

"Don't you think it's too late for games?"

"Absolutely," Sara said, that tartness back in her tone.

He rolled off the table, then reached for his shirt. She wanted to take her eyes off him, but she couldn't. He looked so darn good, and she wanted him so darn bad, that she had to fight the urge to fling herself into his arms.

She didn't, of course. However, their eyes continued to hold as he slipped the shirt on and began buttoning it. Even when he unzipped his jeans to put the shirttail inside, she couldn't avert her gaze.

A new round of color surged into her cheeks.

"It's a little late for that, too, don't you think?" he asked in a husky tone.

Her bones melted on the spot. "I—"

"Oh, come on now, you've seen me with no clothes on at all."

"You get a kick out of embarrassing me, don't you?"

He grinned. "I get a kick out of you, period."

Sara had to do something to get things back under control before *she* lost control. Abruptly Alice's words leaped to the forefront of her mind in neon colors: *He's a ladies' man, always has been and always will be.* "How 'bout Alice? Do you get a kick out of her, too?"

"Ah, so you are sore?"

"I'm *not* sore."

"If your mother hadn't been there, I would've told Alice to go fly her kite in someone else's backyard, preferably her husband's."

"Cute."

"I'm serious," he said, leaning against the table and crossing his arms over his chest. "I'd much rather have spent the evening with you."

Realizing that Alice was no longer a threat, Sara should've let Clark off the hook. Yet she couldn't. Alice's warning just wouldn't go away, which added to her mistrust.

Sara swallowed hard. "Look—"

"You believe me, don't you?"

His heated words forced her to meet his eyes again. "I don't know what to believe."

For a moment he turned away and faced the window. Her eyes followed his, and she watched a muscle twitch in his jaw before she gazed beyond him and noticed that dusk was fast approaching.

They were alone now, she knew, having heard Rosa slam the back door.

"Why didn't you tell me you'd never been with a man?"

Sara's knees threatened to buckle. "I...you... didn't ask."

Clark turned around, and though his eyes still smoldered, his lips displayed an indulgent smile. "Well, that's not exactly something you ask a woman, you know."

"You're right, it isn't," Sara admitted without enthusiasm, feeling as if she was wading in water totally over her head. If she wasn't careful, she would sink.

Where she wanted to sink, God help her, was down on him, feel him high inside her again like a spear. God! What had happened to her? Had his hands and lips turned her into a sex fanatic?

"I'm sorry if I hurt you," he said in that same husky tone.

"You...didn't."

"Then why wouldn't you talk to me afterward?"

She ignored the growing tightness in her chest. "For all the wrong reasons, I would imagine."

"I was afraid you were sorry, that you wished I'd never touched you."

Her bones melted another degree. "No, I don't, didn't, wish that at all."

He was quiet for a moment, seemingly content just to look at her, which elevated the sexual chemistry crackling between them.

"Did it bother you?" Sara put a hand to her flaming cheek. "I mean—"

"I know what you mean," he said softly. "And no. It made me feel quite special."

This time she couldn't find any words to respond. They were all clogged in the back of her throat.

"Look, we need to talk," he said at last.

She smiled a lame smile. "I thought that's what we were doing."

"We are, but not under the best of conditions."

"What do you suggest?"

"That we go somewhere and grab a bite to eat, then go from there."

She wanted to ask where, but didn't. Instead, still stalling, she asked. "What if I'm not hungry?"

He shrugged. "You never are, but I am."

Why the hell was she fighting herself and him? She ached to be with him. "Let me freshen up, then I'll be ready."

He moved closer, then reached out and ran a finger down one side of her cheek. She steeled herself against the onslaught of need that invaded her system.

"I'll be waiting," he said thickly.

Down, boy, take it easy.

Clark took his eyes off the street and glanced at Sara. She was staring straight ahead, toying with her lower lip in an obviously nervous gesture that burned him like wildfire.

But if he wasn't careful and didn't mind his manners, he'd be spending the remainder of the evening alone, the area below his abdomen smarting like hell. Throughout dinner she had behaved like a skittish colt who had been broken, but was still unpredictable, who had to be handled with TLC.

He was trying real hard to behave. What he really wanted was to pull off the road and kiss her until she couldn't breathe.

Just thinking about that made him hard. Good thing it was dark in the vehicle, or she could probably see that he was about to burst through his zipper.

"This isn't the way to my house," she said into the silence.

Clark glanced at her again. She was watching him through wide-set eyes, her lips slightly parted.

Beckoning.

"I know," he said when he could get himself back together.

She opened her mouth as if to say something, then slammed it shut again.

A few minutes later he pulled into the drive at his aunt's house.

"What's this all about?" she asked.

"I thought maybe you might like some coffee."

"Here?"

He chuckled. "Why not? You didn't have any at the restaurant."

"That's because you didn't give me a chance."

"I'm giving you one now," he said in a low, gravelly voice. "So what's it going to be?"

Clark waited while the silence of the night throbbed around them with much the same intensity as his body throbbed.

"It's still early," she said without looking at him.

"I'm assuming that's a yes."

A cricket chirped close by.

"You assumed right," she said in a small and quivering voice.

Clark's gut tightened, but somehow he managed to get out, then open the door for her. Moments later they were inside the house where a light from the hall cast the living room in a muted glow.

That was as far as they got. He looked at her and she looked at him. Before he realized what he was doing, he had her backed against the wall, pinned with his body.

"Clark!" she gasped. "What—"

"You know what." He kissed her then, hot, savage kisses that sent the blood soaring to his head, making it pound.

She moaned, kissing him back.

"Is this the flavor of coffee you serve?" she asked in a breathless voice after he removed his lips.

"Yeah." He ran his finger over her bottom lip. "Do you like it?"

"It's my favorite." She trapped that finger in her mouth and sucked, never taking her eyes off him.

He drew in his breath, then blew it out. "Mine, too," he whispered.

"So what now?" she whispered back, blowing her breath on his lips.

He rubbed his groin against her. "Room service."

"In the bed, I presume."

"You got it," he ground out.

"This was what you had in mind all along, wasn't it?" Sara asked, moving in rhythm with him, like dancers in concert.

Clark felt sure the top of his head was going to explode along with another part of his anatomy if he didn't hurry up and end this erotic foreplay.

"One way or the other I was determined to have your hands on my body."

"So your back wasn't really hurting?"

"My back was hurting. Along with something else."

"You're bad," she whispered, reaching down and putting her hand on the bulge between his legs.

He jerked.

She froze.

"Don't stop, please." He heard the agony in his voice but couldn't temper it.

She rubbed some more. "You're *real* bad."

"What I am is horny as hell, but then you know that."

He heard her labored breathing, but he didn't know if it was a result of what he'd said or the fact that he had unbuttoned her blouse, unclasped her bra and had his mouth locked on a nipple.

Her head lolled back, and she moaned, "Oh, Clark."

When that nipple was sufficiently laved, he moved to the other one.

"I feel that down to my toes."

"I want you to feel it here." His voice was hoarse as he undid her slacks, and once they were pooled around her ankles, he slipped a finger inside her lace panties.

She moaned, then squirmed. "Please!"

He picked her up then and carried her to the bed. As before, clothes were frantically cast aside, and only after flesh was against flesh was Clark satisfied.

"Take me now," Sara said, her tone pleading.

Wordlessly Clark parted her thighs and entered her. With no barrier this time, he thrust deep and high.

She clutched at him even as he rolled over, taking her with him.

"Clark?"

"It's all right. It's even better with you on top."

She stared down at him, wild-eyed, when he closed his big hands around her breasts, and she began to move.

"Oh, yeah, that's it," he said in a strangled voice when she upped the pace.

But her journey was short-lived. They both climaxed hard and fast, their cries overlapping as she collapsed on top of him.

He didn't know how long he held her or stayed inside her. Time suddenly seemed meaningless. Though she had fallen asleep, he hadn't. His mind was in too much turmoil.

"What are you thinking about?" she asked after a while, having rolled off him.

Now was the time to tell her why he was there and what he wanted, he told himself, facing her and pushing her damp hair off her forehead. But for whatever reason—he didn't know—the words wouldn't come. It was as though his throat was paralyzed.

"Clark?"

"Uh, I was thinking how beautiful you are and how much I want you again."

She held out her arms, which exposed her breasts and turgid nipples to his gaze. "You'll get no argument from me."

Groaning, he leaned over and began sucking.

Sixteen

Don't get your hopes up, Sara Wilson.

She had told herself that all the way to Quiet Haven. But she did have her hopes up, especially after last evening. Clark cared about her; she just knew he did. No one could make love with such passion, such brazen intensity, such stamina, and not care.

Or could they?

The problem was she didn't know that much about men and their sexual appetites, nor did she want to. As far as she was concerned, the only man she'd had was the only man she wanted, now and forever.

In the short span of time Clark had been in town, she had become addicted to him and his body. And vice versa. He'd become addicted to her, if his actions were anything to judge by.

Or was that the way he behaved with all his women?

A sick feeling invaded her stomach, but Sara refused to give in to it. Was it possible for them to have a future, or was she being played the fool like Alice had said? She knew Clark, yet she didn't. She had seen both a hard side and a soft side. Which one was the real Clark? Right now she didn't know, and she didn't much care.

Each time they were together she fell more in love with him. But was that love hopeless? She couldn't make that call; only Clark could do that. So far he'd been mum about his private feelings.

There were so many factors against them she didn't want to face: she was older than he was…while that might not bother him, it bothered her; he had already been married, and unhappily, at that; and last, she didn't fit into his world and didn't want to. And he didn't fit into hers. He had left and wasn't ready to return to small-town life. She had left and couldn't wait to return.

But again, the most important ingredient missing on Clark's part was love. She didn't even know if that word was still in his vocabulary.

All she knew was that when he left, not *if*, her life would never be the same again. She would revert back to the quiet, serene routine of work, looking after her mother and the nursing home, things that were once enough to fulfill her.

Now, after experiencing another side of life with

Clark, she realized how empty hers had been and would continue to be once he had gone.

Yet she wouldn't take anything for their time together and would cling to those memories forever.

By the time she pulled her car into the nursing-home lot, Sara was smiling, and it felt darn good.

"Mornin' boss," Edwin said as he came out of the cafeteria.

"Good morning to you, too."

Edwin stopped in front of her. "After you make your rounds, do you have a minute to stop by my office?"

"Why don't we go there now?" Sara paused. "Unless it's not convenient for you."

"No problem. Come on."

Sara followed him down the hall, wondering what this was all about. It could be any number of things. Running a nursing home was one of the most stressful and time-consuming jobs known to man. And because she, rather than the Merricks, took an active role in overseeing it, she bore the brunt of all the problems. But then that had been, and still was, the way she wanted it.

Whatever the matter, it could be fixed. Having Zelma disappear had been the worst-case scenario, and they had survived that, only because Clark hadn't raised hell. If it had been any other family, Quiet Haven would have had a suit slapped against them.

Sara shuddered to think about such a thing happening in light of the fact that it would heap more financial burdens on her, not to mention what it would do to the nursing facility.

Thrusting those thoughts aside, Sara preceded Edwin into his office and sat down while he closed the door.

Once he was sitting behind his desk, he faced her, a frown lining his forehead. Sara shifted in her chair, feeling uneasy.

"How well do you know Clark Garrison?" Edwin asked without preamble.

For a moment Sara was so taken aback that she couldn't answer. Forcing her expression to show nothing, she finally said in calm, cool voice, "Why do you ask?"

Edwin's eyes flicked off her, then back. "He called me the other day—" He broke off and cleared his throat.

"He called you?"

"Yes, he did," Edwin said emphatically

Sara felt a sinking feeling in her stomach. Had she been wrong about Clark, regarding the nursing home? Was he going to take legal action after all? If so, why hadn't he said anything to her? It didn't make sense.

Sara voiced her thoughts in an unsteady tone. "Is he going to sue us?"

Edwin looked confused. "Sue us?"

"Yes, as in a lawsuit over Zelma?"

Edwin shook his head as if to clear it. "No, at least not that I know of."

Sara went weak with relief. "Thank goodness for that. You had me worried."

"Well, I'm still worried," Edwin said flatly.

Sara's eyebrows arched.

"Clark Garrison is interested in *buying* the nursing home."

If mild-mannered Edwin had dropped a live grenade in the middle of the room and it had exploded in her face, Sara couldn't have been more stunned.

Sara opened her mouth, only nothing would come out.

"I'm shocked, too," Edwin said in a dull voice. "That's why I asked how well you knew him. Evidently, you didn't have any inkling of this, either."

"Buy Quiet Haven?" Sara repeated in a faraway voice filled with total disbelief.

"That's what the man said."

Sara stood, albeit on wobbly legs, then stared at Edwin through dazed eyes. "This facility is *not* for sale."

Edwin rose to his feet, his mouth stretched in a grim line. "I hope you're planning on telling him that."

Sara felt herself rally almost as quickly as she'd gone down. Her eyes flashed fire. "Oh, don't worry. I intend to. Do I ever."

Love.

The worst-case scenario had come to pass. He'd fallen in love with Sara, something he swore wouldn't ever happen to him again.

Clark was at the ranch, having just come from the north pasture where Joe was repairing a line of broken fence. He'd wanted to help, had even been tempted to, but Joe had flatly discouraged him. Deep down he knew Joe was right.

Too, he could envision Sara's disapproval, so he backed off and observed. But he was getting tired of pampering his back. Hell, he needed physical exercise to knock some of the demons out of his mind.

Sara. Sweet, innocent Sara.

Loving her had not been in his plans. Even though he'd taken her virginity, he had thought he could just walk away when the time came without looking back and without regrets.

He now knew better.

Yet he was committed to doing his job, even though it would hurt Sara in the process. God, he hated it when his conscience reared its ugly head. Rarely had he had a problem with that.

Loving Sara had changed things, changed *him*. Although she had never told him, he knew she loved him, too. He had seen that love in her eyes and heard it in her voice, though she had tried so hard to keep him from knowing.

He loved Sara and he loved his job. And they were on a collision course. But all was not lost. He would figure a way out of this mess and make it work. He wasn't about to give up Sara, nor was he willing to give up his work.

He would invite Sara to the meeting with Turner and the Merricks, be up-front with them all. If she loved him, and again he was sure that she did, they could work something out.

Feeling better, Clark brushed down his horse, then walked out of the barn only to pull up short. Sara was standing on the back porch of the house.

His heart leaped at the sight of her. "Hi-ya!" he called, waving his hand and heading up the hill, for once, his gait showing he was free of pain.

She didn't respond.

He stopped in front of her and shoved back his Stetson. "My, but you look fetching this morning."

"You bastard!" she spat.

His eyes narrowed. "What?"

"How dare you?" she spat again.

She knew. Damn Edwin Turner for not keeping his mouth shut. He'd like to strangle the administrator's scrawny little neck. Instead, Sara was here to strangle his. That was what he got for not keeping *his* mouth shut until the appropriate time.

Clark lumbered up the steps, but didn't dare get too close. It was obvious Sara was furious. Her entire body was trembling. Damn! "I was going to tell you."

"No more lies!"

"Look—"

"No, you look. Go back where you came from. Today."

Clark shook his head. "It's not that easy."

"Oh, yes it is."

"If you'll just give me a chance, I can explain."

Sara laughed then, a half hysterical, half ugly laugh. "You're something else, you know that."

"Sara, please."

"That's why you screwed me, isn't it?"

Clark blanched. "No, dammit, it isn't."

"Liar!"

"If that's what you want to think, then fine. But it's not true."

She looked him up and down with loathing. "I don't believe you."

"I know you don't, but I aim to fix that."

"Sorry, but it's unfixable."

Her voice dripped with sarcasm, yet he sensed she was close to tears. He had picked up on that slight crack underlying her words. It was all he could do not to grab her and hold her close, plead with her to hear him out. But he knew that wasn't about to happen. No telling what she'd do if he tried to touch her now.

"I work for a company that buys and sells nursing homes."

"And you...they want Quiet Haven." Sara's voice was devoid of emotion, like someone else was talking.

"Yes."

"What about the Merricks? Have you already spoken with them, behind my back?"

"No," he said tersely.

"But you intended to, right?"

He stalled, trying to find the words that would vindicate him and save them.

"How could you, Clark?" she said in a broken voice.

"Look, it would be for the good of all parties, especially you."

"Just what does that mean?" she lashed back.

"You'll get out of debt. You're in way over your head financially with the home."

Sara gasped. "Dammit, have you been spying on me?"

"Unfortunately, that's part of my job."

"Well, you can take your job and go straight to hell!"

"Sara, don't." He heard the pleading desperation in his voice but couldn't control it.

"Oh, just one more thing," she said. "Why Quiet Haven? I know it's special, but it's not that special."

Clark felt himself turn green, but he wasn't about to fudge on the truth now. Besides, if he didn't come clean now, all would definitely be lost.

"Oh, never mind," she said fiercely. "You'd just lie some more, anyway."

"There's plans to put an interstate highway through here."

Her eyes widened. "God, you are a rat."

"Sara—"

"No! Don't say another word. Just listen. I'll never put my name on that piece of paper. And know, too, that I'll never forgive you for betraying me like this. But most of all, I'll never forgive you for using me."

"Please, Sara, don't say that."

She laughed that nasty laugh again. "Why the hell not? It's the truth, isn't it?"

"No, dammit, it's not. I love you."

"Oh, that's beautiful," she said backing up as if she couldn't stand to be anywhere near him. "Really beautiful."

He felt blood rush into his cheeks. "There's something else you have to know."

She gave her head a savage shake as she continued to back up. "No! You've said enough. I don't want to hear any more of your lies."

Ignoring her, he inched forward. "I'll admit that when I hit town, doing my job was all I had in mind. Hell, as far as I was concerned, one nursing home had always been the same as another—buildings, nothing more, nothing less.

"But that changed when I visited Quiet Haven. I realized that it isn't just a building, but rather a home for people like Zelma and your mother. And Sam. God, what would happen to him if he didn't have the facility?"

"I wish I could believe all that, but unfortunately I don't."

He cursed silently. "I know you're upset right now, but maybe later—"

"There won't be any later, Clark." Sara's spine was straight, and her voice was as cold as icicles. "I could never trust you. And love without trust is as worthless as it gets."

"It's not over yet, Sara."

"Wrong!" she fired back. "Don't come near me again."

With that she turned and walked off the porch. Clark watched until she got in her car and disappeared. Feeling as if all the air had been drained out of his lungs, he grabbed one of the posts and leaned against it.

But his mind raged. He had to do something to make things right. Unexpectedly he knew what that something was.

He dashed inside the house, picked up the phone and punched out his boss's number.

"It's Garrison. We have to talk."

Seventeen

She should have known better.

If something sounded too good to be true, it usually was. Why hadn't she paid attention to that old truth? Why had she let her heart overrule her head? Why? Why? Why?

Sara lurched off the sofa and walked to the window. It was Saturday, and she hadn't left the house all morning. She figured Katherine was wondering where she was, as she usually spent most weekends at Quiet Haven with her mother and other residents.

Not today.

No way would she punish anyone with her mood. A death row murderer would be more company than she was. While she was angry at Clark, she was furious with herself. Again, she should have known better than to get involved with the likes of him.

Emotional suicide.

That was what she had committed. She couldn't forget the physical part, either. Now that she had experienced his touch, experienced the sweet agony of physical pleasure, she would never be the same again. When Clark had kissed her that first time, he had uprooted her world. She would never be able to replant it.

Give it a rest, Sara.

She couldn't. She couldn't stop thinking about how he had used her to get what he wanted, which was the nursing home. Well, she had news for him. He'd get it over her dead body.

She had tried to call the Merricks, but they hadn't been at home. She had left a message on their service. What if they were meeting with Clark? What if he convinced them to sell?

Her panic burgeoned, then subsided. They wouldn't do a thing like that, not until they contacted her. While they weren't nearly as involved in the facility as she was, they were proud of it and wouldn't want to see a corporation own it.

Sara shuddered. She had seen homes where the owners had sold out, and immediately the quality of care sank as quickly as paper down a flushed toilet. Quiet Haven, she vowed, would not suffer that kind of fate.

But what if money talked? What if the Merricks wanted or needed the money? They couldn't need it any more than she did, that huge bank note looming forever large.

Still, she wouldn't consider selling her share in the facility, not even to another individual. What she would have to consider, very seriously, was returning to Dallas three days a week. She didn't dare miss one payment.

Damn your hide, Clark Garrison.

The sad part about it was she still loved him. Yet she hated him, too, if that made any sense. His betrayal had cut her to the core. If only he had been up-front about why he had come to town. And while there was no excuse for his behavior, she couldn't place *all* the blame on him, though she hated to admit that.

She was an adult, a grown-up who'd had the right to tell him to go away and leave her alone when he'd first come on to her. But she hadn't. She had thrived and blossomed under his attention, especially after he had introduced her to the world of sexual passion.

Suddenly, Sara's face flamed and the walls seemed to close in on her. She had to get out of there, do something, anything that would take her mind off her heartache or else she was going to lose it.

Newt.

She would go see him. As always, he was the perfect antidote for her puny heart.

Five minutes later she was sitting on his sofa sipping a cup of coffee. He seemed to sense right off that something had her in a high snit. But instead of mollycoddling her, he muttered gruffly, "You look like bloody hell."

Sara's mouth curved down. "I feel worse than that, actually."

He didn't say anything until he emptied half his coffee cup. Then he pinned her with the same intensity as a scientist peering into a microscope.

"So what's got you down in the mouth?"

"I bet you think I'm awful."

"Why would I think that, girlie?"

"Because I always run to you when something's wrong."

He smiled. "That's what keeps this old ticker ticking."

Sara jumped up from the sofa, crossed to where he was and kissed him on a prickly cheek.

"Ah, don't get all syrupy on me. Just tell me what caused your latest bellyache."

Though he brushed her affections aside like they were pesky mosquitoes, Sara knew he wallowed in the attention, all the more reason why he shouldn't be living alone. One day, she *would* get him to Quiet Haven. She just prayed it was still while he was in his right mind.

"Go on, spit it out," he encouraged.

"Remember I mentioned Clark Garrison to you?"

"Yep. And I encouraged you to go out with him."

Sara stretched her full lips into a grim line. "That's another story in itself, one that I'll save for another time. What I will tell you is that he's in town to buy Quiet Haven."

˙ "Well, I'll be damned," Newt said, scratching the whiskers on his chin.

"Supposedly he works for a corporate giant that preys on little companies, mom and pop operations, until it beats them down or puts them out of business."

"And you're madder than a wet hatter."

"That's mild compared to how I feel."

"What's the special attraction for a company like that? Oh, I know the facility's one of a kind, even though I don't want to live there. Still—"

"Greed. Pure and simple. Eventually an interstate highway's going through this area. Did you know that?"

"Nope. But you need say no more. The property value around here will shoot straight up."

"Exactly." Sara's voice was trembling with suppressed anger. "And it wouldn't surprise me if they were to get their hands on Quiet Haven, they would tear it down and put a shopping mall there."

"Did he say that?"

"No, but I know how these companies work. They don't give a damn about people, just money."

"So what are you going to do?"

"Whatever it takes to keep Clark from getting his hands on it."

Newt was silent for a moment, though he didn't take his gaze off her. "You love him, don't you?"

"Yes," Sara choked out, fighting tears.

"It wouldn't do for me to get my hands on that son of a bitch about now," Newt said fiercely. "I'd tear that young whippersnapper in two like he was a twig.''

In spite of pain churning inside her, Sara smiled. ''And I'd let you, too.''

''Uh, that remains to be seen,'' Newt mumbled.

Sara struggled to get a clear breath. ''Isn't this pitiful? Aren't *I* pitiful?''

''The answer's no to both questions.''

Sara's eyes filled with tears. ''What am I going to do?''

''What do you wanna do?''

''I don't know,'' Sara wailed, her eyes blurring with tears.

''Well, I can't give you any advice. That's something you'll have to figure out for yourself.''

Sara was still mulling over those words of wisdom a while later, after she had returned home. She loved Clark, would always love him. But could she forgive him?

He had said he loved her. Sara grabbed her stomach, hoping to stop it from churning. Earlier she would have given anything to have heard those words of love. Her heart had ached to hear then. Now it was too late. They were meaningless. Or were they?

When push came to shove, wasn't love more important than a building? Of course it was. But it was Clark's betrayal that she couldn't get past. So where did that leave her?

Sara shuddered.

Was it possible somehow to compromise? Could love be the salve that healed? Should she listen to the dictates of her heart? If not, then she deserved the fate of being alone for the rest of her life.

Was her pride worth that?

"Thanks, Lance. You're a prince of a fellow."

"I just hope it works out for you, man." He paused. "And that you know what you're doing."

"I hope so, too," Clark responded into the phone. "Keep me posted."

"Will do."

Once that conversation was over, Clark released a long-held sigh of relief, then got up, only to turn around and stare at the phone. Should he call her?

No point. When she heard his voice, she'd slam the receiver down in his ear. He didn't blame her. He blamed himself. He took full responsibility for screwing things up between them.

If only he'd told the truth from the get-go, they would be together this minute, most likely making love. But more than that, he would be telling her how much he loved her.

Feeling as though his brain was boiling, Clark rubbed his temple, but the gesture was futile. Somehow he had to see her, to make her listen to him. How?

Then it hit him. *Voilà!* Why hadn't he already thought of that? Moving faster than he'd moved in a long time, he headed out the door.

Five minutes later he was at the clinic, giving Rosa a kiss on the cheek.

"Oh, my goodness," she said in a hyper voice while grinning from ear to ear.

"You won't regret this."

"I'd better not," she said, her eyes sparking and the grin gone. "I don't have to tell you how special Sara is."

"I know," Clark said softly, then turned and strode into Sara's vacant office.

When she walked in a few minutes later, she pulled up short and gasped.

Clark held up his hand. "Please, before you kick me out, *hear* me out."

"Give me one good reason why I should," she whispered, her face drained of color.

"Because I love you."

She visibly sucked in her breath.

"And for another, I convinced my company to put their money elsewhere."

Her eyes brightened, yet the shadow of mistrust remained. "How did you do that?"

"It's rather involved."

"I have plenty of time."

"Well, I sold my shares in the corporation, then used that money to buy out the Merricks."

For a moment Sara looked winded, like she'd just had all the air punched out of her lungs.

"Does that mean—" She stopped mid-sentence as if unable to go on.

"Yep. *We*, you and me, now own Quiet Haven,

and it's not up for sale.'' He paused and ventured closer to her. "Right?''

"Uh, right,'' she whispered in a dazed voice.

"So how 'bout it?''

"How about what?'' she asked, still whispering.

"Marry me.''

Clark grabbed her then, and before she could speak, he adhered his lips to hers. He knew the answer when she melted against him and returned his kiss with added fervor.

Then he pushed her away so he could see her face. "Am I forgiven, my darling?''

"More than that,'' she said breathlessly, "you're loved.''

Epilogue

"**M**mm, that feels good."

"Do you think our son likes it, too?"

Sara propped herself up on her elbow and watched as Clark planted more kisses over her rounded stomach. "I wish he'd like it enough to make his presence known in this world."

Clark grinned, then kissed her on the tip of her nose. "Don't rush my kid. He'll come howling down the chute when he's ready."

Sara slapped him on the arm. "You're awful."

"And you're lovely, Mrs. Garrison," he said huskily, moving her closer against him, "especially now that you're having my child."

Sara let out a sigh of contentment. The word *hap-*

piness couldn't begin to cover how she'd felt since she and Clark had married, a week after he'd conned himself into her office.

The wedding had been a family and community affair, having been held in the flower garden at the nursing home. Newt had given her away, but only after she had bullied him into moving to Quiet Haven.

Since Alice had returned home to her husband and children, Rosa had been her attendant. Sam had stood up with Clark, which had tickled the old man.

The lawn chairs had been filled with friends from River Oaks and Dallas, and residents of the facility. Since then Sara's life had changed to such a degree that she didn't even recognize it herself, especially when she learned she was pregnant.

To her delight Clark had been delighted. While he still worked for the corporation part-time, traveling to Houston every so often, it was with a completely different attitude. He had become nursing-home friendly, which in turn served the company much better.

Soon, though, he planned to retire to the ranch, where they now had a house under construction. Until it was finished, they were living in her small house, readying themselves for the birth of their son.

Sara couldn't wait, nor could Clark or her mother. And the event was due within the month.

"What are you thinking about, my love?"

Sara snuggled closer. "Our baby."

"Do you miss work?"

She pulled back and gazed at him. "Sometimes, but not enough to try and massage someone, with my paunchy tummy."

He tongued a nipple and she moaned. "Except me, that is."

"I'll work on you anytime, anywhere, mister."

"So how about now?" His tone was strangled.

Her eyes sparkled. "Which part of your bod needs my attention?"

"This part," he said, grabbing her hand and placing it on his chest, at his heart. "Think you can put those magic fingers to work on me?"

"Oh, yes, for the rest of your life," she whispered.

Clark's eyes darkened. "Is that a promise?"

"It's a forever promise, my darling."

*   *   *   *   *

If you enjoyed what you just read,
then we've got an offer you can't resist!

Take 2 bestselling
love stories FREE!
Plus get a FREE surprise gift!

LINDSAY McKENNA
continues her heart-stopping series:

Coming in October 1999:
HUNTER'S PRIDE
Special Edition #1274

Devlin Hunter had a way with the ladies, but when it came to his job as a mercenary, the brooding bachelor worked alone. Then his latest assignment paired him up with Kulani Dawson, a feisty beauty whose tender vulnerabilities brought out his every protective instinct— and chipped away at his proud vow never to fall in love....

Coming in January 2000:
THE UNTAMED HUNTER
Silhouette Desire #1262

Rock-solid Shep Hunter was unconquerable—until his mission brought him face-to-face with Dr. Maggie Harper, the woman who'd walked away from him years ago. Now Shep struggled to keep strong-willed Maggie under his command without giving up the steel-clad grip on his heart....

Look for Inca's story when Lindsay McKenna continues the MORGAN'S MERCENARIES series with a brand-new, longer-length single title—coming in 2000!

Available at your favorite retail outlet.

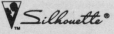

SDMM2

SILHOUETTE®
Desire®

continues the captivating series from
bestselling author **Maureen Child**
BACHELOR
BATTALION

Defending their country is their duty;
love and marriage is their reward!

December 1999: **MARINE UNDER THE MISTLETOE**
(SD#1258)

It took only one look for Marie Santini to fall head over heels for marine sergeant Davis Garvey. But Davis didn't know if he was capable of loving anyone. Could a Christmas miracle show him the true meaning of love?

Don't miss Silhouette's newest cross-line promotion,

Four royal sisters find their own Prince Charmings as they embark on separate journeys to find their missing brother, the Crown Prince!

Royally Wed

The search begins in October 1999 and continues through February 2000:

On sale October 1999: **A ROYAL BABY ON THE WAY**
by award-winning author **Susan Mallery** (Special Edition)

On sale November 1999: **UNDERCOVER PRINCESS**
by bestselling author **Suzanne Brockmann** (Intimate Moments)

On sale December 1999: **THE PRINCESS'S WHITE KNIGHT**
by popular author **Carla Cassidy** (Romance)

On sale January 2000: **THE PREGNANT PRINCESS**
by rising star **Anne Marie Winston** (Desire)

On sale February 2000: **MAN...MERCENARY...MONARCH**
by top-notch talent **Joan Elliott Pickart** (Special Edition)

ROYALLY WED
Only in—
SILHOUETTE BOOKS

Available at your favorite retail outlet.

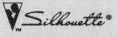

Silhouette®

Visit us at www.romance.net

SSERW

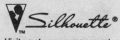

Start celebrating Silhouette's 20th anniversary with these 4 special titles by *New York Times* **bestselling authors**

Fire and Rain
by Elizabeth Lowell

King of the Castle
by Heather Graham Pozzessere

State Secrets
by Linda Lael Miller

Paint Me Rainbows
by Fern Michaels

On sale in December 1999

Plus, a special free book offer inside each title!

Available at your favorite retail outlet

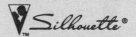

Visit us at www.romance.net

PSNYT